I0747847

Passageway

Edited by
Sam Agar,
Paula Dias Garcia
and Marc Clohessy

Sans. PRESS

LIMERICK, 2023

Passageway
ISBN: 978 1 7391383 3 2
Published by Sans. PRESS
July 2023
Limerick, Republic of Ireland

Cover Artwork & Illustrations by Monge Han
Layout & Book Design by Paula Dias Garcia
Typeset in Calluna and Alverata

Editors
Sam Agar, Paula Dias Garcia and Marc Clohessy

www.sanspress.com
@PressSans
sans.press
/sans.press

Collection © Sans. PRESS, 2023
Individual contributions © individual authors, 2023
Cover artwork © 2023 by Monge Han
Reprinted with permission of the illustrator.
All authors and artists retain the rights to their own work.

Passageway receives financial assistance
from the Arts Council.

Editor's Note

*Paula
Dias
Garcia*

At first, the plans for our fifth anthology seemed to centre around a single, if complex, question: *what lies beyond the doors of transformation?* Would it be a new world, or a new person crossing it? Would it be beautiful, or terrifying? Or, even better, both?

And, to our continued surprise, our writers seemed all to be in agreement. The answer we received, again and again, was resounding: *well OBVIOUSLY, behind the door there is another door.* Change can hardly be ascribed to neat boxes, with tidy *before* and *after* labels; really, what is out there is the constant state of transformation, a flow that moves through and around us, and challenges us to alternately swim with it or dig in our heels.

The question, then, seems to change by its own accord. Once this knowledge is nestled in your chest – *the doors will be never-ending* – it becomes about how you prepare for them; and here the answers vary wildly.

It becomes about what you decide to bring with you, and what to leave behind; about what *can* be carried with you, and what is way too heavy for the journey. About who is ready to hold your hand along the way, knowing that change will come for them too, and who cannot admit that the door even exists.

It becomes about accepting the nature of transience of all things – both staying still and moving forward will bring its own consequences. It's not, then, about *whether* you would like things to change, but *how*.

And though each of us will carry different things through these doors – burdens and gifts alike – in the end, there's always the question of how much of ourselves to carry through. In every story, we found the loving generosity of memory, of leaving behind enough of ourselves for those who love us to hold, but also the resilience of keeping that which we can't give up without losing ourselves.

It's such a tenuous line, and each writer in *Passageway* threads it lightly – the challenge of becoming who you will be without losing who you are, of moving forward without abandoning the past. Choosing yourself, while still loving the world.

It has been such a great journey, and we're grateful to everyone that allows us to keep following where these stories go. To every single writer that sends us a story, to the booksellers, to the Arts Council, to all of our readers – thank you for keeping the paths open.

Behind this door there is another door, and behind that, another.

The Paths

Content Warnings

A Haircut's Not For Scaring You: mental distress, death of a loved one (mentioned), death of a child (mentioned);

Loveliness: stalking, mental distress, death (poisoning);

Infestation: childbirth;

Home For The Rising Sun: discussions of suicide, car accident (mentioned), racism (referenced);

Happy Seedful Day: queerphobia (implied);

Acid: sexual content, mental distress, illness/death of a family member (mentioned);

Limbo: mental distress, suicide attempt (mentioned), illness of a loved one/family member;

Transition Island: injury detail;

The Trees: suicidal ideation, violence, death of a loved one, death of a child, large scale death (implied);

Don't Dig Her Up Again: sexual content (mentioned), pornography, long-term illness, death of a loved one;

Spectro: sexual content (mentioned), injury detail;

This Is About Art: mental distress, self-harm (mentioned);

Birthday: death of an infant (mentioned).

*"Think you're escaping
and run into yourself.
Longest way round is the
shortest way home."*

**– James Joyce,
Ulysses**

*"The great revelation
perhaps never did come.
Instead there were little
daily miracles, matches
struck unexpectedly in
the dark; here was one."*

**– Virginia Woolf,
To the Lighthouse**

A Haircut's Not for Scaring You

Emily Iseult Duggan

The door blew in like an Atlantic swell. The moment my arm touched the surface, it *swung* round its hinges to clatter up against the burgundy wall. Tadgh's eyes rose up to meet me. He was down on his knees behind a young man's head, his arms cast, with hair taut in his left hand and a comb in the other.

I turned around to check that I was there. My feet were still in boots and my body clothed. I grated my face with those scratchy gloves, passed them over my brow bones and beard.

When I turned to face the room again, Tadgh was back at the young man's hair. He hummed out of his chin with half his head scrunched into itself. His movements were sagacious, like Tai Chi, slow and rhythmic postures between gusts of his wrists.

I set myself parallel to the wall. I was so wound up leaving that I'd forgotten to bring something to read or look at. If Anna was here, we'd be playing games. I spy a mirror, razor, cashbox, scanner, scissors, set of rollers. I listed out things that I could see.

Chair, floor, hairdryer.

Cup, lightbulb, hand.

Young man.

Tadgh.

Drain, brush, magazine.

Computer, clock, leg.

Tadgh slapped the young man on his shoulder. The young man twisted his jaw around his head, trying to see the back of it in the mirror. He pulled the sheet that was tucked into his collar and tufts of his rusted hair were sent flying round the room. They hovered, catching the yolky light that was seeping through the window. For a couple of seconds, they were like confetti, or bits of shattered glass.

'Marcus, I'll be withyah in a minute.'

Tadgh shuffled to his counter.

The young man jerked, as if he hadn't noticed me come in. He pivoted round and looked relieved to see that I was nothing worth noticing anyway.

The young man pressed his hand to the scanner and Tadgh thanked him when it shrieked. He strode down the room to the door and it bulged open again and shut closed.

Street.

Shoes.

Clouds, car, umbrella.

'Marcus,' Tadgh lowed.

He looked old all the way over there, from this side of the room. I went over to him. He carefully watched me come. I held my forearm up to the scanner and it yelped out again. Tadgh drummed his fingers on the wooden countertop.

'Come'ere and we'll let this load.'

The screen lay a blueness on his face. It made it droop, made his eyes sink lower into his flaccid cheeks. He took a breath that slowly caved his chest into his neck.

'Right,' he said. 'You can suí síos anseo.'

He made his way over to the seat adjacent to the one the young man had sat in. The second from the right as you're looking at the mirrors, fourth from the left if you're facing the wall. I sat down there in front of myself, and Tadgh took up the sheet and shook it out like a beach towel. His broad fingers inched the brink of my shoulders as he tucked it into my neckline.

Nose.

Frame.

Jacket.

'Well, then, Marcus, will we start with the face or the head, so?'

'The face, Tadgh.'

I examined the scribbly thing I'd let wild on my face for the past few years. It was thick as shrubbery, knotted and murky. It was a long time since anything had passed through it. If you dared to put your finger in, you'd expect it to be thorned and dusty on removal.

'She's some feat, the depth of her.' Tadgh pinched the hair between his fingertips. 'She must be some time in the making.'

He knew right well how long it was in the making. Sure, wasn't everyone all over me at the beginning? Dropping in, bringing dinners, things for the freezer, flowers. Hugging me and patting my back and looking me in the eye and telling me it wasn't my fault. That *please God* things would get better, that Anna and Deirdre would be ok, that they were together at least.

Bottle.
Radiator.
Window.
Cobweb.
'Aye, Tadgh.'
He unzipped his tool case and pulled out his scissors.
'We'll have to snip her first before we shave her, alright?'
Shelf, shower head.
Plug, tap.
'Aye, Tadgh.'
'Snip her, like cut her off, Marcus, yeah?'
When I looked up, I could see the worry shooting up through his throat and out of his eyes like a fountain after the sight of me. Ach, don't people just run kind? Aren't they only trying to do their best to you after all?

I threw my elbows out and heaved my body up. Tadgh stepped back.

'Ah, now Marcus, it'll be grand. Where on earth are you gonetuh?'

I slid back on my scratchy gloves.

'I'll be back in a few, Tadgh. I'll just have to get the garden shears.'

His expression eased slack back into a smirk. He exhaled through his nostrils and dabbed at his belly.

'By God, you nearly had me, lad.'

He set himself to my haircut then, tilting my head back in the chair with his gentle, worked hands. He hummed again as he looked through that beard of mine. I said you could spin wool from it – he asked me if it was the beard my gloves were made of.

Tadgh laid a damp towel over my eyes. It was doubled and wet and warm. It spread itself in past my skin and all around to my temples. It felt nice at first, but there was something that perturbed me about being in the dark. Instead of seeing, I felt my insides going. The more I felt, the worse it got. My eyeballs gyrated round behind my forehead, gaining speed the longer that they spun. My jaws fell into oscillation. My teeth clamped down on my cheeks like they were sawing them through. Underneath, my bare neck was all cold and exposed up to the ceiling. As I sat there, and Tadgh flittered his scissors around my jawbone, my neck stiffened itself in a dreadful arch above the ridge of the seat. As the sound of Tadgh's steel fingers spun clicking, the back of my neck continued to contract, my Adam's apple pushing up like a hatching egg. I couldn't breathe. I choked.

'Marcus! Marcus!' Tadgh's hand lifted my head and did away with the towel. He placed my hands on my stomach and instructed me to breathe.

I looked out at the room around me.

Tile, cement, drip, skirting board, rail.

Wall, corner, wall, corner, ceiling, light, mirror.

Chair, chair, chair, chair, chair, Tadgh.

I caught my breath then.

'I'm grand now, Tadgh.' I said to him without looking.

Ceiling, leak, strip light, plaster.

'You still want me to cut it, Marcus? Are you sure now?'

Cobweb, paint, spider.

'I am.'

'We can leave it at that if you want. I've cut it even as it is.'

Corner, flaky paint, pipe.

'Nah, Tadgh, you can finish it.'

'Are you certain?'

Wire, damp patch.

'Aye.'

He left off the towel this time.

He left it off, which meant that I could see his face, nudging in and out of my peripheries. In and out, over the buzz of the razor. As clumps of sinewed hair fell off me, Tadgh's eyes almost crossed in concentration. The tiniest tip of his tongue stuck to his stringy, aged lips. He hummed breathily. His face was kind. It always had been. He'd been cutting my hair for years now. Mine, and Deirdre's and Anna's. He'd cut everyone's hair in this town. Even when the smart salons arrived, people still came here to Tadgh's place with the peeling wallpaper and cobwebs and lilting chairs; with the same painted shopfront and hinged wooden door. It had been in his family for six generations. You'd be hard pressed finding another business that lasted that long and managed to stay the same. Even when the laws changed, when people started with the chips and scanners, Tadgh's shop was a nook of the way things used to be. You'd never notice the scanner on his oak counter. It was shrouded in the feel of the place. A pragmatist would deem Tadgh's business obsolete in this world, yet there he was, still cutting people's hair – cutting my hair.

The buzzing stopped.

'I'll clean you up after we do your mop, Marcus, alright?'

I raised my head back up straight and looked at my face, almost bare, there in front of me. My peachy chin, my sloping jaw – the things the beard had hidden. My skin was putrid. It looked like it hadn't seen light for months, and I suppose it hadn't.

With that, I felt my stomach clench. Anna wouldn't know me now. That's all I could think when I looked at myself. She wouldn't know this fella. She wouldn't know this pulpy, helpless–

Mirror, wall, chair.

Tadgh.

Scissors, bottle, apron, comb.

I swallowed.

'Aye, Tadgh.'

'Right so, Marcus.'

Tadgh pulled up a brush. Then he took up a hand mirror.

'I'll show you here, what we have, Marcus.'

He held the mirror so I could see the back of my head.

'You see the way it's a bit tangled?'

I saw it. It looked more like a wild animal attached to me than tangled hair. It barely resembled human hair at all.

Fingernail, ring.

Knuckle.

'Now, the reason I'm showing you, Marcus, is that the tangles don't matter a tap if we're going to shave it off. If that's the case, I can just hack away at it until it's a reasonable length for the trimmer.'

'Do that Tadgh, cut it off. I don't care how you do it as long as it's gone.'

Tadgh looked me dead in the eye. He continued speaking, slowly and steadily.

'Well, Marcus, if that's what you want, but it would be an awful big change for you. With the beard gone, it's very different already. What I was going to explain was that–'

'No, Tadgh, I want it gone. That's what I booked in for, isn't it? Just get it off me, please.'

He held his shape, waited for me to finish.

'What I was going to say, Marcus, was that I can brush it out. Once it's untangled, I can have a look at it and talk you through our options. Sure, you've always kept your hair a bit long. You've lovely hair, Marcus.'

Hand.

Stool.

Blade.

Wire.

Forehead.

Brush.

Picture.

Cupboard.

Tadgh.

Hair.

Arm.

'Just hack it and shave it, Tadgh. I don't want it anymore. Please.'

Tadgh's eyes pressed on me like two big fingertips. They lingered for a moment. Then he dipped his head and clipped the hand mirror back to his apron. He clawed his hand through a clump of my hair and slid the open mouth of his scissors through it.

I'm not certain what happened next. For all my heedful watching, my eyes were suddenly shut, and I couldn't see at all. Everything else, the feelings and sounds and tastes in my body, were suddenly urgent and dilating, spewing up my throat. With all of my will, I couldn't separate my eyelids to ease the building force. This time I was certain I was going to choke if I didn't–

'Tadgh, it's just,' my voice quivered. 'Tadgh, it's just I'm a bit nervous.'

I said it with my eyes sealed but I saw it hang there in the air. I heard the drag of a stool over the joins on the floor and Tadgh sat down beside me. My insides continued to gush up my gullet and my lips were cranked apart.

'It's not just nerves, actually. I'm scared. I'm scared about it all being gone. My whole head is going to be completely different, and I've never had it without hair since I was a baby, and sure, I don't remember that. Sure, babies don't remember a thing.'

Even the shop's hum seemed to have gone stark.

'Babies remember some things, Marcus.'

My face went into contortion.

'They don't, Tadgh. They don't remember a thing. You hardly remember when you were a baby?'

'Ah, 'tis a long time since I was a baby, Marcus, and truthfully, I don't remember much in the conventional sense of the word. But here's the way I see it, Marcus – I was born a baby, and I grew up to be myself from the baby I was born as. D'yah understand me?'

I squeezed my eyes together, and fists on my thighs. I nodded my head.

'And anyway, Marcus, who says you have to cut your hair back like a baby? You don't have to at all.'

'I do, Tadgh. I've nothing left, and that's a good thing because I can't look after anything at all. I can't even take care of the hair on my head since–'

I crumpled. My head buckled into my belly and my crown to my knees. Everything was dark and wet and something from deep within me shook like a tremor.

Tadgh's hand sat on my shoulder blade.

'Ah, Marcus,' he said. 'A haircut's not for scaring yah.'

⑊ ⑊ ⑊

It must have been an hour or more that Tadgh spent combing out my hair. I didn't watch him. I didn't even ask him to do it, but he knew, in all his experience, what was needed for my head. I kept my eyes closed and I listened to him humming with the room, working away. I left my head lenient to his hands: it moved where he placed it; his fingers pushed around my muscles and teased out the hardened spots.

Tadgh selected the point at which I'd keep the hair above and let go the hair below. The hair he cut off was frayed and dry like kindling. I opened my eyes only at the end when he was finished, and he slapped my shoulder, softly, to let me know. When I opened my eyes, things looked different, but not completely.

I paid with my arm at the scanner, and I left a tenner on the counter when he wasn't looking. I knew it was useless, but it was just for the gesture of it. I put on my gloves again and went down to the door. Before I put my hand on it, I turned round to Tadgh and thanked him. He wished me luck and waved me on.

Out I went, back into the ferocious weather, and the door swung closed behind me. It was dark now, almost night, and the sky returned to brandishing its whirling air at my body. Unlike earlier, though, my hair was permissive to the wind, and absorbed its demands before they could bash against my skull. When I reached my room, it settled in a drape over my head, like it was a blanket, or embrace. I shut my eyes and thought about Anna.

Loveliness

*Raffaella
Sero*

The house will forget us when we're gone.

She told us that; Susan did. Susan who was going to be an architect, so she knew about houses. She knew that houses have short memories and no heart; that student accommodations need to protect themselves. Absorb none of the chatter voices weeping that inhabit them, let everything go. Make themselves numb to nostalgia or else their beams would rot.

We weren't in the house long enough to leave a trace, is what we've come to realise. Thought it would be our home for a year, at least. Then we could move out of college together if we had to, though–

hard to imagine, living away from Whitstead: away from its crooked floors giggling corridors shouting cupboards three floors rancid kitchen ghosts–

hard to imagine but a few months was all we had.

‖‖· ‖‖‖· ‖‖·

Some days,

dead autumn days perched between the real world and the sport fields of Newnham College,

a scarlet bloody rotten trail of leaves will lead you to the door of Whitstead House.

You're not ready for the way it looks at you, the house, back from the shops or from the library or from a run on frozen wet Grantchester Meadows. The yellow flicker of leaves over rain-darkened roof tiles. Its blank stare, unsettling.

I moved in the summer before my final year. Got the email one evening, late, from Newnham admin: a place on college grounds had suddenly become available, and was I still interested, and would I mind letting them know immediately, and surely I could see they had a long waiting list to go through and: the room was in Whitstead.

I hadn't heard the name before, though when I looked it up I recognised the large white house by the tennis court I must have walked past hundreds of times. I'd always assumed it was abandoned.

Newnham website informed me Whitstead was built in the 1930s, that it had two kitchens four bathrooms a living room – the unheard-of luxury of a dining table – seventeen bedrooms. Google told me Sylvia Plath had lived in one of these, for a spell between her undergrad and her marriage.

I emailed back that night and said Yes, when would the room be available? The administration lady said, Immediately.

I arrived on a Sunday: walked in with care unnecessary: outside was dry and warm and the end of term and the house was empty. My room, on the middle floor, one of the smaller in the house, had a fake fireplace, empty rows of bookshelves, dark wooden panelling holding on – unless I imagined it – to the presence of its previous inhabitant. Her smell lingered in the curtains, over the stripped-down bed. (Would mine?)

I'd lined the walls of my previous place (an even-smaller room on Castle Mound, soulless apartment blocks mostly herding roaming roomless international students) with pictures of dead poets and empty buildings. These walls I decided to leave bare; I folded my clothes into the scratched set of drawers, hid my suitcase under the single bed, and ventured into the garden.

That first grey sultry summer afternoon I spent belly down on the grass, reading cover to cover *We Have Always Lived in the Castle*. Above, the sun moving over the leaves moving over my head, in and out of bleached-out clouds and shadow-trees

       from the edges out of sight small creatures creeping in a cat couple of squirrels a deer – utterly unrealistic – bands of black ravens

    marched on grass fluorescent green beneath scorched sky I felt observed, whenever I looked up I'd find the house

       inspecting me from unblinking windows. Eyelids flickered open   garden lost its gleam   cold damp evening grass scratched cheeks awake I breathed in

       gulps of air thick with smoke

      chatter the smell of cooking meat.

Our last summer would be boisterous busy like that evening, a barbecue in Whitstead garden after slow golden days on Grantchester Meadows. We'd slip into the river past Newnham village, past Lammas Land, among mossy bends, bent tree branches, places past places where boats and punts and other people's laughter could find us. We'd slip in shrieking with pleasure though the water was cold and dirty bug-infested full of children's piss. Then climb out of green slimy sludge, fingers buried deep into the riverbank. No matter. At Whitstead, someone would take care of the thick dark half-moons of mud lodged like dried blood underneath my nails, brush my fingertips with a wet sponge, gently-expertly like my whole body was blown out of coloured glass.

Girls were flocking towards me from the skyward-smoking barbecue–

You must be the new girl   Sorry we woke you up, mate
                    You looked so peaceful!
          What's your name?
                              like a princess in a fairy tale
What subject do you do?
          like Snow White
                    Where are you from? I mean
Where's home to you?
                    like a corpse, you mean
                    Don't listen to her; here, have a burger.
The one offering food, porcelain-white and wide-eyed like a doll: I'm Penelope – Penny – I'm in Room 15, she said.

I sat up, passed a hand over my mouth, dried the drool on my fingers as inconspicuously as I could.

I'd gone vegan, hadn't tasted meat in six or seven years; but I took the plate from Penny's hands. I brought the burger to my mouth and I sunk my teeth into it. Probed at the fire-licked bulk of it with the tip of my tongue, believed I could taste running blood. I chewed once, twice, three times. I swallowed.

ılı· ıllılı· ılı·

Not all of Whitstead was in the house when it happened; that's one of the things the *Daily Mail* got wrong.

Take Didi. She was in the library: she was always in the library, when she wasn't reading in her room (which she wasn't on the night it happened; I checked, I'd know.) We hardly ever saw her, never heard her move, not even those of us on the first floor whose ceiling she should have been walking on yet

no footsteps no snoring no coughing no laughing no surreptitious scraping of bedpost against wall

but she was grouped with the rest, whenever we received a noise complaint or the ground floor bathroom got flooded again, her address was on the email so we knew she was still there – probably still there. Probably reading. Eyes to words, words on pages, relentlessly turning.

And there was, or rather wasn't, the girl who never showed up, though we knew she was paying rent because we'd been told no one else could move into the room. So it stood vacant, between Winnie's and Kay's on the ground floor, the whole time we lived in Whitstead. We used to stare into it from the garden, sometimes, using our phones as torches to peek at the emptiness inside, five or six of us even squeezed on the step where you could tell at some point in the life of the house a french door had been walled.

But I was there,
and so was Penny
So were
  Claire

Ali   Rachel Gerry Iris   Mags

Mary Susan Winnie   Kay

As for Rosie and Joan, fuck knows where they were that night. Not in the house. Not at the Virgin Suicides' Last Supper, as people call it on the internet. Those two never used to hang out with us. For all we know, they're still alive.

∿ ∿ ∿

The ladybird invasion started with term, at the end of September.

They crept in with the autumn, colonised every surface of the house, crawled up kitchen chairs

solitary

or pressed together, as though to keep warm, in corners of the

ceilings and of the floors

red drops of blood in the bathrooms

dead on white windowsills: brown and stiff

like coffee beans

pinned onto our ceilings by drafts of cold November blowing through single-glazed windows, they were the house's secret eyes.

We didn't spend much time in our rooms, or out of the house. Whenever we tried to leave, it seemed, we'd bump into someone – in the corridor or on the stairs, or in the laundry room one hand on the backdoor already – and something would come up to keep us in Whitstead. A game to play gossip to exchange food to cook cigarettes to smoke surreptitiously arms outstretched out of the kitchen door　　how do I look can I borrow your straightener will you walk me there text me when you're　　　home.

Whitstead is an old house. A place of steep steps creaking bones and cupboards under the stairs, stuffed with abandoned half-forgotten things. As the days got shorter, we spent longer darker hours sorting through its tatter, like every cupboard was a treasure cove out of the Arabian Nights. Look, a hula hoop

a sewing machine   a ouija board

a broken radio

a complete set of the Twilight novels

the Bible

cutlery plates pots frying pans bent out of shape by time and

heat

And what the fuck is this?

A massive copper saucepan, old-fashioned, too heavy for Mags to lift from the place she'd found it, at the bottom of the bottom drawer of the downstairs kitchen.

A cauldron, what else, Ali said. Will come in handy for the Sabbaths.

A theatre kid, Ali, and they were writing their thesis on *The Crucible.* That's why they said what they said. Just a joke. None of us were witches, or satanists, or (almost) anything the tabloids implied. People will write all sort of things, and believe them too, but truth is what happened at Whitstead is in no way remarkable. Soon it'll be swallowed in a stack of Twitter notifications and everyone will forget about it, about us. Our lives will be just a story with nothing to say but this: death comes cheap. Much cheaper than you'd think.

Today tomorrow alone in company by poisoning fire

hands of a man a lover a friend, in the end

there it is the end, still there still

waiting to happen.

On 18th October, a month and a day before the day we died, Penny in the downstairs kitchen clutched between cold fingers her favourite mug, blowing on her coffee through lips the same size and shape and colour as rose blossoms.

I have boys news, she announced to the room. Her lips unfurled slightly at the edges, upwards, like a smile.

We made a face. Two weeks ago we'd started keeping track of Penny's boys news, in tidy graphs of yellow and blue and red chalk on the blackboard in the living room. Every day, once the data had been collected and analysed

TED	plus 10 points
	(bought Penny a drink)
RUPERT	minus 350 points
	(has a girlfriend who isn't Penny)

we'd squeeze on the couch sagging armchairs carpeted floor for a little round up. We couldn't agree, had it been Mags' or Susan's idea to begin with? But Claire was put in charge of the blackboard because she studied maths and didn't like men.

We kissed.

Who kissed?

Penny's smile bloomed into a peal of laughter.

Me and Ted, obviously!

In came the OOOOOHs and BOOOOOs, hurled through the open common room door.

Fuck, Penny, not *him*

        Yes, Penny, fuck *not* him

  Finally some action   I think he's *kinda* cute

      I wanna know *everything*

        This isn't going to end well.

I forget who said that. Susan or Mags? Ali Iris Rachel or Kay? Could be me.

Could be I never knew; we'd all started to sound like each other, by then.

᠁ ᠁ ᠁

It felt like a lot was happening, around that time; Ted's kiss got lost in lecture experiments classes club nights that stretched till late dawns; it feels like nothing now.

Gerry's throat ached, but what of it she didn't have time to see a doctor, not now in the middle of term

Kay's eyes felt itchy: in the morning she'd find them caked with yellow dust they wouldn't open until she felt like she could

Winnie knitted a scarf for me, then a hat for Penny, then a pair of gloves I know she was going to give her mother for Christmas but she never

Iris had bought a deck of tarot cards. She fell into the habit of reading our future every night, after Claire's analysis of Penny's dating life. (It never seemed to us that Iris was lying, though of course she must have been; or if she really saw our future, she did nothing to change it.)

Ali was directing *Heathers: The Musical* at the ADC Theatre. Most of Whitstead was involved in the production. Kay designed the lights, Winnie the costumes, Susan the set. Mary, Rachel and Gerry played one Heather each. Penny was Veronica: I got a haircut and leather jacket and went for Jason Dean. No room was safe to walk into, you'd find someone singing stepping counting out of time muttering trying to convince themselves they're

a good person big fun just back from hell

like hell's your parents' house, or the South of France or Italy after the summer, somewhere you can come back from at the beginning of term, with a tan.

And all that (lovely) while

blue bugs bleed black blood black bugs blue

twisted our tongues around the house.

There were nights after rehearsals, rainy and interminable, when wind and water like hands – impatient – slapped every window in Whitstead, flew all eyelids open. Some nights we shuddered ourselves to sleep, alone in our beds.

Some nights we ventured for comfort into the corridors, groaning floorboards drowned by downpour underneath our naked feet.

Doors opened

and closed, quiet like secrets too obscene for the telling. It was one of those storm-beaten nights I found her, shivering raindrops from her curls onto the wooden steps leading to the top floor.

Together: Are you OK?

I

had been on my way to Claire's room.

Blinked a couple of times. Must have been sleepwalking, I said. You? Are you OK?

Penny's hair was a heavy, dripping mass. It flew about her face, raining more water onto the steps, too fast to know whether she was nodding or shaking her head.

Ted was there tonight.

There? I asked.

At the bar crawl.

Ah. I. Thought it was just Newnham–

It was. Supposed to be, I mean. Maybe I. Maybe I, mentioned it to him? I don't know.

I sat down, stretched an arm around her shoulders.

Her eyes, not looking at me, opened so wide I thought I could see them glint. A fox, off-guard, in the middle of a night road. I could feel the water on the steps soak through my nightie, at the back of my thighs. I didn't move.

He was, Penny started eventually, and again: He was. Hovering. Just behind me. The whole night. In the first bar

          and the second

    and the third he

        didn't come to talk to me, she added quickly, I told him that I. He knows I don't want to see him but still

        he was just

               there.

He'd been just   there   for some time now, long after his name had disappeared from the blackboard graphs of Penny's boys, long after the long awkward walk to Grantchester during which Penny had told him she didn't want to take things further ('couldn't you walk him around Newnham gardens? how long does it take you to break things off with someone?') he had just   kept   being   there.

Pressed against my arm, Penny's neck twitched.

When I walked into the living room the next morning, every name number coloured line had been carefully erased from the blackboard.

Already I can feel us fading

and (isn't it strange) already I don't remember anything before Whitstead.

I know I must have been somewhere, before being here: if
I still had eyes I could squeeze them into the thick mist just
across the doorstep of my consciousness:

remember.

This much I remember

Whitstead existed for me, had been meant for

foreigners outsiders Sylvia Plath when

she wrote in her journal that day

a dream was planted: England: here it was

But where was I?

Where was

I

(there are many ways to haunt a place only one of them

is to let the place haunt you)

She called the house her sanctuary: when she said she
wanted to go home Whitstead was the place she meant though
she – Sylvia – was only here a few months,

the house shall forget us when we're gone

unless the house isn't even here anymore isn't even

but where is here if not Whitstead?

In the end we were too scared to use the ouija board.

We'd have a game night instead, we decided, in Susan's
room which was the biggest. Some of us sat on the wooden

benches built into the walls. We passed a few garden chairs through one of the windows, to squeeze around the old rickety three-legged table–

That's why it moves, Claire promised. It's broken that's it that's all.

One of her hands was squeezing one of mine, fingers inter-locked underneath the table. She reached her other hand to the top of my head, when she took it back a ladybird was strolling on her finger, red and black like a game of roulette.

We played Monopoly that night and Pandemic and Cards Against Humanity. We didn't want to go to bed, but then it was the Box's turn and it said:

Ghosts + Friendly fire. = Nothing good
happens after 2 a.m.

We stopped playing after that.
In bed,
we tried to force our eyelids down but the darkness
wouldn't let us so we stared on at it
– pitch black starless – on and on and on until it wasn't
it was
bright loud screeching breaking the night like an eggshell.
Empty bellowing hurled like curses from the ceilings opened eyes all through the house fingers flew to phone screens: 3:33 a.m.

Once we'd stumbled out of bed – into coat and shoes, out of rooms – the screeches became loud enough to hear over the fire alarm.

What the hell

It's upstairs, it's–

Wake up! Wake UP!

Just   get   out

someone get the fire blanket, quick

like that's going to do anything!

the flames were high for moments they enveloped Claire's desk

completely

so hot on my cheeks it made me want to laugh but I didn't. I was the one who got the fire blanket when Susan told me to. I threw it on the desk and the fire was gone. It left the night cold and a heap of black charred paper dust floating in the air.

By the time the porters made their way through the gardens and across the sports fields, Claire's desk had been cleaned up and a story found. Oil fire: we got distracted frying eggs: the kind of thing that happens all the time in student accommodations.

Mark the head porter has been doing his job for almost thirty years; he knew better than to question the fact we'd been cooking eggs after 2 a.m. He didn't frown, didn't tell us to be more careful, didn't look puzzled at the smokeless kitchen: just asked, in the driest possible tone, Everyone alive?

(Like a god, Mark enjoys the gift of utter indifference to the affairs of students. The only time I saw something like discomfort cross his face was on the night we died.)

Mark gone, most of us climbed back to Claire's room, in procession to the top floor and down the long white doorless corridor.

Room 14, Sylvia's old room: one of the smallest in the house so some of us had to wait, standing by the open door.

I must have fallen asleep, Claire kept repeating, mantra-like, when she spoke at all. Mostly, she remained tight-lipped. Hugging her knees for comfort on top of the unmade bed, her eyes looked like they wanted to fly away from her face, looked

like they never wanted to meet mine again.

Still Susan found the heart to scold her: Whitstead is made of wood, almost entirely of wood what were you thinking one

spark and it could go up in flames like a house of cards–

She wasn't thinking she was asleep didn't you hear

And the fire started itself, sure.

I don't know what happened but I know it doesn't help to shout at each other

Who's shouting seriously who is, I am just saying

we could have all just died tonight, would have died if–

Sylvia must be watching over us, Penny suggested, a faint smile stretched tiredly across her face.

(She looked tired, around that time, around her eyes, every day I saw her, even though she mostly stayed in her room. Sometimes working, often crawled up in her bed staring up at the ladybirds staring down at her.)

Either Sylvia is watching over us or the ladybirds are really fucking lucky.

Oh my GOD guys it *is* just like that old rhyme, isn't it? *ladybird, ladybird fly away home your house is on fire your children shall burn*

That's cheerful, Mary said.

It's not meant to be cheerful.

And what is it meant to be? A prophecy?

It's not how it goes, anyway: it's actually *ladybird, ladybird fly away home your house is on fire your children are gone.*

Cause that's better.

YES it is because because *because* they're gone, get it? Like, there's nothing to worry about. The children don't burn can't burn cause they're   gone.

Gone where though

Away

Away where?

To a happy place.   Like, IKEA.

Ha-ha. You're hysterical

No, no, but she's right – there are more lines on Wikipedia, too: *All except one, and that's little Ann/ And she lies under the girdle stone.*

Amazing. HA! That's not creepy at all.

How's this for creepy – irrepressible smirk on Ali's face as they went on – *All except one, and that's Sylvia Plath/ Lighting a fire under your bed.*

Stop it Ali

                Oh Claire, it's just a *joke*, I was just

                                Well don't

It's fucking chilling

It's disrespectful

It doesn't even rhyme.

It's true that in the weeks before we died Claire was reading a book about poisons.

I took it up once, while she was showering. I opened it at a random page, and that's where I first read about verdigris, the sea-bright green patina which can form on copper kitchen utensils and kill you. It seemed appropriate that something so lethal should have so beautiful a name,

a name like a spell to keep a princess in a tower.

Gerry was also reading constantly, in those days. A novel, by Helen Oyeyemi: *White is for Witching*: she told us the novel's haunted house, like Whitstead, was on a street called Barton Road.

Spooky, Mary said, without moving her eyes from the scarlet nail polish she was applying to Penny's toes, naked on the carpeted floor in front of the sofa.

Penny didn't say anything about the book. Her eyes followed Mary's hands, seeming to drink in every blood-drop of nail polish.

I think you need to be really *really* upfront with him, Iris said – not for the first time that night – bringing the subject back to Creepy Ted. She was supposed to be reading my future, but I don't think, cannot imagine in all honesty, that she was paying enough attention to the tidy maze of tarot cards spread between us on the table.

Not that simple, Penny rumbled.

A collective sigh. Cooing. Swearing. Had been here before, right here in this argument, all of us.

I just– I don't understand why he won't– leave me alone. Doesn't he get it? How can he not get it? I haven't been replying to his messages I haven't been speaking to him at the lab I don't sit in the common room at lunch anymore.

He says I'm the only person he can talk to.

He says he knows we are made for each other.   But   why? But

how does he know? I don't want to be
made for him I don't want to

be made

for anyone.

We nodded, saddened into silence. We'd been here, too.

⁃⁂⁃

One week before we died, as we walked back together from the dress rehearsal of *Heathers*, Ali had a panic attack.

Nothing to do with the play, as far as they could tell. Nothing to do with anything, in fact, except the fact that it was 6 p.m. and dark, and that darkness had long fallen and that it falls every night

every night it falls black and strange and frightening
– Ali tried to explain later, eyes focused, small and dark
like the dead bodies of ladybirds –
strange and frightening, too, that we never say how strange and frightening it is.

If we admitted to ourselves, like children do:

yes, I fear that the light will never return
yes, I know there are terrors that crawl in the night
yes, *fuck* yes, I am afraid of them horrified half-out of my wits
then we should all go mad; but how much more reasonable, to go mad.

In the kitchen, I passed Ali another glass of water, as I nodded and I nodded. I wanted them to know I understood, but I couldn't risk to open my mouth just then. Sparks flying around a bonfire, my thoughts just then, soaring too close to the tip of my tongue: windborne insects fluttering in the darkness.

If we could– just stay in Whitstead, all the time, I said. The darkness is all outside, you know. Like. It can't come in here.

Ali smiled the smallest saddest smile: We can't just stay in Whitstead. Not forever.

On the evening of Ali's panic attack – the same moment, perhaps, when they were sitting shaking on the wet pavement on Sidgwick Avenue – Susan saw a man standing by the house. She was walking homewards, an orange plastic bag glowing in each hand: in the dim rusty light of the one lamppost on Barton Road, it wasn't easy to tell whether the man's floppy hair was gold or bronze, his coat green or blue. When he saw her coming he jumped back onto his bike, cycled away, too fast for Susan to see his face – not that she'd have recognised him, she said later to me   She'd never met Ted.

Maybe it was a Deliveroo driver.

Without a backpack?

Susan told me the story in the laundry room, as we were spraying Ziran into its mouldy corners. The anti-mould was supposed to be poisonous only if injected, still Susan made us wear masks and behind the blue-white fabric I couldn't decipher her expression when she said: Don't tell Penny about this, OK? It'll only frighten her.

⫶⫶⦚⦚⫶⫶

Penny's birthday was ~~the last day of our lives~~ on the 19th of November.

A dinner to celebrate. Balloons. Pink paper garlands in the common room. None of us liked clubbing, anyway, except for Penny herself. She was sick, by then, of leaving the house sick

of being constantly escorted   of   constantly   having   to check over her shoulder   for the tail of Ted's green raincoat,

for a glint of his golden round glass frames.

After erasing the boys' point system, the blackboard in the common room remained empty until we started selecting a Quote of the Day.

Things we said, or our friends said; things we overheard on King's Parade; random things random people said to us on dating apps:

so, books are a thing for you

why do you want to be lifted you're not a cat I guess I'll pay for whatever they do to me

welcome to the unhappy middle

insanity is so close I can almost touch it

A group of ladybirds is called a loveliness : this quote stayed on the blackboard for three days before the dinner. We never thought of checking its accuracy, because it meant that Whitstead was full of loveliness and that made perfect sense.

We made risotto out of the frozen entrails of the pumpkins we'd carved for Halloween. Earlier that evening, Penny and I had picked herbs from the winter beds in Newnham gardens. Surrounded by the 4 p.m.-drowsy redbrick buildings in the blood-orange sunset. We filled the wicker basket I bought last week from Oxfam for £1.50, balanced it on the windowsill in the kitchen. By the time we poured the herbs into the risotto, they seemed to have increased in volume and strangeness; like they'd kept growing, with a fairy-tale trick, long after we'd cut them.

⼁⼁⼁ ⼁⼁⼁⼁ ⼁⼁⼁

At 6 p.m. Ali helps me heave the copper cauldron onto the sink. It's the first time we use it: I wash it with a soft sponge. I decide
the bright green film that dresses its inside
is too beautiful to scrape clean
so instead I cover it, cover the bottom of the cauldron in a thick white layer of arborio rice. Like a secret, like a spell.

The window above the stove stays open, to let the black night in; and in it comes, in gusts blowing clouds of vapour against our cheeks as we take turns to stir.

When their turn comes, I take a video I shall never post on Instagram, of Ali chanting to the rhythm of the circling wooden spoon:
ladybird, ladybird fly away home your house is on fire
your children shall burn

Is it still a loveliness, if all the ladybirds are dead?

Wild Animals

*Anna
Martin*

It's as if they are alive, this family. This young girl, me, aged twelve. As if we might spring out of this yellowing frame and live again. Not that we are dead. I'm certainly not, anyway. But there's something about an old photograph that reminds us of how far we've come. They say the body is renewed every seven years, every cell different. I've been more than three different people since then, since I was the girl in this photo, standing on the hill in the sunshine wearing a handmade floral shift dress.

When I think back to that time of my life, it is always summer. It is too hot, it is dusty enough to choke on, my thighs rub each other red. Inside the house, small windows keep the worst of the heat out but let the dust in, the dust and the flies. And the dust and the flies stick to whatever they must: grease on the cooker, sweet spills under the table, drying batter in the bowl.

The photo, too, has its cycle. It appears and disappears to its own schedule. When I want it, when I'm grasping for something to remind me who I am, it won't be found. And at times like this, when I'm moving on again, when it helps to forget, here it is, amongst the chaos. Such a small object that if you turn it sideways it almost vanishes. But sometimes it's the small things that matter, that linger: these things fit in a palm, in a pocket, these are the things that you take with you. My family will have their own small objects that help them remember what only they can.

The woman who took the photo is a stranger.

'Leila,' she said, 'means dark, or night.'

So, let's start here, at the end of one thing and the beginning of another, at the things we'll agree on: an orange kitchen, a dead wasp, the smell of flour in the heat. And with the girl, with me, aged twelve, in the house on top of the hill.

⫴ ⫴⫴ ⫴

That morning our routine was broken by a knock at the door, scratchy like there was an animal trying to get in. Mother got up and gave her who-could-that-be look.

In the space where she was, dust fell in a shaft of light from the window.

There was mumbling in the hallway and then, as clear as a bell: look-who-it-is! And there was now a stranger standing in the doorway of our kitchen. I looked but did not know who this stranger was. I would never know who she was, not really. The stranger stood with one hand clutching a plastic cup of blue ice and the other flat-palmed on the door frame. She had soft, golden-brown hair and a small pink bubble of gum retreated into her lipsticked-mouth. She wore a white t-shirt with a plasticky picture of a sunset over a beach. Pulled tight across her chest it said: *Florida*.

The stranger said, 'hi.'

I said, 'hi.'

But it did not sound like the stranger's 'hi', which went up at the end with a big *e* sound. I practised the big *e* under my breath until my brother kicked me under the table and mother said, did-you-hear-what-I-said? I closed my mouth and nodded. The stranger smiled. Her smile was a bright flash in the room. The stranger did as mother said and came in, sat down. She swung her small handbag over to her left and dropped it on the floor. On her fingers were a row of big, bright rings: a pink gem heart, a turquoise egg, a thick silver ring stamped with the figure of a bear up on its hind legs.

I looked at the stranger. She was sucking her blue ice through a plastic straw. Her face was wide and brown, and she had pink lips and blue eyes. On her eyelids was blue powder that was like fishes in a sunny pond. She smelled like coconuts.

My brother sat opposite me at the old greasy table and played with a wasp under a glass. He held the glass so tight his fingertips whitened and he moved the glass in and out, in and out, and each time he was in he trapped a leg, and each time he was out the leg was not on the wasp anymore. The wasp sound got higher. I closed one eye.

Mother was talking so fast it was like bubbles coming out of her.

'–not-a-part-of-our-lives-anymore,' she was saying. She placed her warm hand on my head. The name my father gave me, Calista, hung in the air. 'Anyway,' she said, 'that's why we call her Callie.'

My brother snorted. He didn't like to hear about our father, and he didn't like that I was named after a bear, and he was named after a small bird. I sometimes imagined us wild in our animal forms, breaking free of this place and making our own way into the world beyond the top of our hill, him small and fluttering at my great furred shoulder with his grim mouth elongated into a perfect little beak.

Mother poured tea from the white teapot.

The stranger held her hand out under my face and pointed at the ring with the bear on it. She smiled and said, 'far-out.' Then she opened her small handbag and took out a lipstick. She pressed her finger into the pink and rubbed it on her lips.

Mother smiled at me. Her favourite song, Maggie May, played on the radio. She was leaning against the blue kitchen cupboards. The kitchen cupboards were the blue of the summer sky. The kitchen walls were orange. Her apron was blue too, with full lemons and sharp green leaves, and it was pulled tight around the waist so some of the lemons were warped and misshapen. Her smile was ancient and sharp and knew everything: not-to-worry.

Lunch that day was late, as usual. The more absorbed my mother was in her cooking, the more chaotic it seemed from the outside. Her hair was coming undone, there was flour on her sleeves, flour in the air, and the kitchen was splattered with the burst bubbles from the pot. The room smelt of heat, yeast, and woody herbs. She fanned the flies away with yesterday's newspaper and smacked them into the countertops where she could. In the corners of the counter, garlic cloves shrivelled or burst with green shoots and the hard, savoury rubble of old bread mouldered. She stirred the soup with her strong arms and ladled it out into a mismatched selection of bowls, none of them completely clean. Deep red dripped over the counter tops.

Mess like this was a part of our lives. My mother was, probably still is, a messy person. She was blind to dirt and grime. Here she is, smiling for the camera, her sleeves rolled up, her apron with lemons and leaves, a dusting of flour across her cheeks. I have never been good with mess, at least not since I've known any different. My own kitchen is white and inside the white fridge are the things I need to keep me alive, lined up and stacked neatly in the cold light. It is hard to keep a place clean, I know that now that I am grown. And there is no denying it: this place is a mess. The cases are open and the cupboards are empty, my life is scattered on the floor in front of me. Moving gets worse before it gets better. It always seems like such a simple task – I've done it so many times, it may as well be in my blood – but it's a slippery thing and always takes more from me than I remember.

Still, this is my life, and I have built it alone. I look around my apartment now in wonder at the order I have wrought on the materials I was handed, at how far I have come. My apartment is clean and bright, twenty-four stories up. I am closer to the sun here, closer to the gods, if you like. Around me, my things. I bring with me what I can carry, two cases and little else. Into this case: Cat, a large and luxurious cat too big for this place. One day soon I will set her out on some pavement in the rain and let her go and live her life, but for now she is mine and I am hers. Into the other case go the things I hold on to: a vase from Mexico, a bracelet from Vietnam, some books to inspire the path ahead, my favourite lipstick: *desert rose,* and the photo. These things are a comfort to me when I have arrived at wherever it is I'm going next, old and worn though they are from the journey. They help me settle, like butter on Cat's paws.

⑊⑊⑊

Mother put a bowl in front of each of us and asked if we wanted bread.

The stranger said, 'thank you, Helen.'

The words pulsed between my ears.

Thank you, Helen.

Heh Len.

My brother watched me frown.

I have convinced myself that this was the first time I had heard my mother's name. This was when I understood that the world she shared with me was only one world, perhaps one of many that she inhabited.

She opened the oven and steam rushed out.

Usually during mealtimes we ate well, and quickly. We would throw crusts and balled-up napkins at each other as we slurped and chewed. We would mouth words: pig, ugly, fatso. But on that day, we did not. Even my brother was complicit in this stunned but elegant silence and, when the stranger asked him what his favourite subject was at school, he was able to quite eloquently say, 'I would say, science.'

But rather than enjoy the new peace and order, my mother seemed uncomfortable. The lines around her mouth twitched. She fussed over us, wiping soup from our faces or patting flour out of our laps. She looked at her children longingly, as if we were only partially there.

She was wise, my mother. Is, probably, still wise.

The room was finally still, the plates empty. My mother pushed her chair back and returned to her stove, my brother picked up the dead wasp and touched it briefly to his tongue before dropping it in the soup bowl.

There were homemade biscuits for dessert, with coffee for mother and, I noticed, for the stranger. The coffee was deep and black and the steam from the cup smelt like caramel and cupboards. My mother dipped a biscuit into her coffee and watched it collapse, soft and heavy, into the cup.

I asked if I could go outside, and mother said yes but stay-where-I-can-see-you. Outside, a cat waited. My dress did not have any pockets and even though I had asked mother to sew some on, she said that I'd only keep secrets in them, and the pockets never appeared. So, I lifted up my dress and took out a biscuit I had put in the waistband of my knickers. I held the biscuit out for the cat who nudged it with her nose and then took the whole biscuit down to the ground. She ate the biscuit like it was made of broken glass. When I touched her head, she flickered inside her fur.

I went over to the look-out. From this corner I could see what was coming. Sometimes the air was misty and I couldn't see very far, but on this day I could see a long way. The biggest buildings were in the city, but they looked the smallest to me. The first time I went to the city I saw that the buildings were giants and their concrete-encased windows shone white, blue, yellow in the sunshine. There is a version of this story where I dropped my ice-cream and cried so hard I was sick, but I only remember watching a one-footed pigeon peck the cone with its grey beak in the shadow of a policeman's domed hat.

The second time I went to the city was on the day this photo was taken, the day I ran away from home. And from the eternal summer days of my childhood I found myself dashed into what felt like the first storm I'd ever known. Do you know what it's like to be in rain like that? After a while the rain becomes a part of you and you just keep on falling down from the sky and soaking into the ground which turns to mud at your feet, and you fall and fall. All you see and feel and know is that motion and the globs of water that cover your eyes and eat your tears and the numbness of your body which tells you you've been washed away completely.

But the girl in the photo doesn't have a clue about any of that, not yet.

Here I am, in my floral dress. I am laughing as a feral cat wriggles in my grasp, pushing its corners into my soft flesh in a bid to be wild again. It's funny, the meaning that rises to the surface with time. I have spent many hours looking at that day in my mind, tracing its trajectory and picking up these threads of meaning as I go. But as I have grown older I have realised that my family, too, will have been tugging at those threads from the other end. Tugging across oceans, continents, tugging, perhaps, from beyond the grave.

On top of the hill I took a big stick and stabbed it into the ground by the damson bush where it was soft. I thought it a good place for a flag so that the cars would know I was there. Mother would say, it-isn't-nice-to-spy. When the summer was over the damsons would fall and burst on the ground, but it was still summer then. I stood there every day and had done since I was old enough to stand. There were three houses at the top of the hill, and to get there the cars took the grey road all the way from the city, then the orange road to the top. They came this way to cut a whole crescent moon out of their journeys when they went to what mother called the posh-people-holiday-homes. They stared at me. I had seen on TV what happens when people drive past real-slow and roll their windows down: Pap! Pap! But that's just the movies and anyway, I felt strong and was really-tall-for-my-age. Inside the cars were the posh-people and they were going to their holiday-homes and they were bringing their perfumes and lipsticks and sunglasses and they were going to sit on their terrace and do nothing-at-all. Absolutely-nothing-at-all. They were like the smell of plastic right out of the box, I thought, like shoes with shiny leather, like ladies' powdery faces: these people were perfect. Even when they were loud, they seemed soft. And they drove past me, and the babies pressed their chubby hands on the glass and the mothers kind of smiled and frowned at the same time and the fathers looked straight ahead. But this time the windows were dark and all I could see was my own small face and – what-has-happened-here – wild hair and some orange dirt from the road smeared across my forehead. The car went over the hill. Another one gone. I felt big.

⑾ ⑾ ⑾

I have often wondered what I would say to that girl if I had the chance now. Do you think I should tell her to be brave? Tell her stories of adventure, stories of growing up fast like she always wanted? Well, it depends. Sometimes I feel her presence and she's crying, wailing, really, and I can't make it all better. But sometimes she's dancing with her arms looping through the air, the little floral shift that mother made hitched up unnoticed. These are the times she's most like me.

Now, of course, I am Calista, although I am often told that I do not look like one. What could that mean? I look in the mirror now and no, I do not present as a wild animal anymore: I wear a three-piece linen skirt suit in a colour that Americans call *oatmeal,* with brassy cones for buttons that suggest something eastern and ancient. My shoes are square-toed and shiny, my hair is sharp and short and perfectly in place. So, I can say for certain that, outwardly at least, I have not become the bear. But there are traces of my family in my face. I have my brother's pale eyes. Now that I am older, I understand my brother more. I wish I could tell him that, and that I often think of him. He was clever, and this will have protected his looks from the days of wasps and perimeter-pacing. His insides will not have rendered him awkward with too-long limbs and a narrow, sullen face holding large teeth. No, his eyes will be the same: grey, dazzling. Perhaps he is by now a family man. Perhaps a businessman. I imagine that perhaps he is the manager of the bank behind a sweeping mahogany desk. An impassioned pastor with a micro-phone-headset. A sweary chef with a pigeon's puffed-out chest. In any case, in my dreams his skin is golden and clean-shaven and there is not a speck of fluff on his long wool coat.

⦁⦀⦁ ⦁⦀⦀⦁ ⦁⦀⦁

There was a big *e* sound and I looked back towards the house. The stranger was standing by the door and waving my sandals in the air. She started marching over and was shouting at the same time, but the breeze took her words.

She was smiling. My sandals dangled from one finger. I snatched them and squinted at her through the bright sun.

'Don't tell your mother,' she said, taking a cigarette and a green lighter from inside her t-shirt. She lit the cigarette and looked straight at me.

I asked if I could have some and she laughed.

'Leila means dark,' she said, 'or night, or something.' She pushed the dirt on the ground with the front of her platform shoe. 'But I like the bear thing, that's far-out.'

'Thanks,' I said, something new and glowing in my chest.

I asked Leila what else she could keep in her clothes, and she laughed again.

'Pretty much anything.'

I hitched up my dress and pulled the other biscuit out from my knickers. I held it out in my palm.

Leila looked at the biscuit. She smoked her cigarette then dropped it and rubbed it into the orange road. Then she took the biscuit from my hand and slid it down the front of her t-shirt. Then she held out her hand and I shook it.

Mother called from the house.

Leila smiled at me, and I felt a rush of summer breeze.

'Better put your shoes on, I guess,' she said.

'Yeah', I said, 'I guess'.

⁂

So, this is it. This is where the photo is taken. This is the end of my childhood. And it is too soon, because at twelve we do not crave the ruptures we might at, say, fifteen. Look at my face, there. Do you see what I see? Something a twelve-year-old girl cannot see? Someone said to me once that desire is simply a mechanism for survival. Look at the photo: all these people are trying to survive. Desire propels us, forces us forward, it squeezes us out. Whether we get what we thought we wanted is luck, chance, and beside the point. We are all bound to a path that bends with our desires.

⁂

Mother fussed and tugged us into place. My brother whined. The cat came looping around my ankles and I picked her up, my mother was too conscious of looking her best to mind. I looked around and Leila was not with us. I felt colour slide. Then I heard her voice, and she was there again, striding out of the house with her camera in her hands.

She stood in front of us with her legs spread wide, the outer edges of her platform shoes pushing up the orange dirt road, and raised the wide, white camera to her face. The cat wriggled and pushed against me. Cats are sensitive.

Leila pressed the big button and caught the photo as it whirred out of the camera.

I dropped the cat. Leila set the camera on the ground, stretched her arms up towards the blue sky and raised her face to the warm sun. She fanned the breeze with the photo. Her top pulled upwards showing a navel framed by a flower with black and pointed petals. *Florida* twisted over her breasts. Her stomach was smooth and brown and her jeans were blue. There were tiny gold hairs on her skin.

She was beautiful.

I remember feeling slack. Soft and sudden. Like the first damsons under bare feet. Like a cake when the oven is opened too quickly. Like running down the hill really fast.

The trees behind her were dark and thick with green. I thought of the biscuit, under her t-shirt, hot in the blazing sun.

My mother touched my cheeks with the back of her cool hand. She was gobbling, garbling, bubbling with words, fussing over my face, her eyes full of laughter. My brother watched with a curious smile.

Leila was saying something but I only heard one word: Helen.

The sun was bright. Mother's soft rounded belly, the creases around her mouth, the halo of frizz on the top of her head loomed in, all of it a trap where there was once comfort. I wriggled in her arms. I swallowed against tears I couldn't understand. The wide-open space I knew so well shrunk around me; the breeze dropped.

I clung to something I knew, swear words my brother had taught me.

Fucking apron, fucking lemons.

But the words remained unspoken.

⊪ ⫼ ⊪

Here there is a gap between one world and the next. I do not remember. Perhaps the straightening of clothes, a comment about the weather, a yawn or a scratch. And then we were trouping back into the dark house and Leila pushed the photo into my hand. On it, our image rose to the surface and began to turn from grey to orange.

⊪ ⫼ ⊪

Leila picked up her things: her small handbag, her pink lipstick, her camera. She tucked a kitchen chair under the table. And she left, backwards, blowing kisses into the room and repeating what I now understand must have been, 'ciao.'

If, at this point, I was scared, I do not remember it. I do not know when the decision was made or if it came from my mind or my body. My mother's palm held out flat towards the yellowing ceiling for what seems like too long, her mouth puckered in a kiss. Then – and this cannot be true – her face, pale, her eyes wide with horror. She looked into me as I sat there dazzled by the new dawn of a thought.

And then she turned away, back to her stove.

⫶⫶⫶

Someone told me once that your eyes do not see the blur of the world as they pass from one scene to the next, or else we'd all be motion sick all the time. But that's all I remember of those next moments: blur and sickness. The roar and clatter of a chair pushed back and over, bare feet gripping the greasy, sandy linoleum, the radio playing on, the door stood open and the brightness beyond like death before me. The blur is my own, the sickness hangs above me like the disappointment of watching gods, and whilst it eases it has never left me.

And then I was outside with the photo crushed in my hand.

Leila. I see her so clearly, standing on the dirt path with the view of the city in front of her, her heels scuffing up the dust. She turns and smiles at me over her shoulder and her mouth is broad and pink.

But I know this did not happen.

By the time I had burst out through the front door there was no one there, not even any dust in the air to show that she had been. I stood on the top of that hill on my hind legs and sniffed the air, grunted at the afternoon sky. Ahead of me, the city.

Infestation

*Henrike
Lehmeier*

A parasite is defined as an organism living inside another, deriving its sustenance at the expense of its host.

Three months I spent horizontally stretched out: on my bed, on the carpet, on the dirty kitchen floor – incapacitated by morning sickness. Stomach turning at the pungent smells of this stinking flat. The downstairs neighbour's cooking in the curtains, the reeking fridge, the sickening scent of the landlord's bathroom soap. Limbs weak, head spinning, like the frenzied bluebottles banging against the rooflight above, I lay sweating in the mid-summer heat, while you sucked every speck of nourishment out of me.

When Mum came over to serve her revolting ginger tea, she was visibly shook by my sorry state. Hadn't herself and Dad done so well setting everything out for me. She had been so proud to show me off: privileged, bright, top marks in carefully chosen senior-school subjects that paved the way to university;

the outlook of my scientific career aligning nicely, prospective titles, publications, international distinctions... Naturally, the disappointment weighed heavy when her hopes were cut short, and me barely through my first undergraduate year. Even her desperate attempt at cleaning up the kitchen would not hide the obvious. Nobody wore baby bumps around campus.

'And just like that–' she snapped her fingers, 'you throw it all away.'

Thankfully she had plenty of neighbours who brought her tea and biscuits to support her through this difficult time.

The parasitic infestation typically harms the host through nutrient depletion or structural damage to cells and tissues, resulting in disease, and often death of the host.

'Let's get rid of it,' Danny said. 'I looked it up, they'll send anything from the States. It's a hundred and sixty-six dollars plus postage. We'll split the cost.'

It turned out surprisingly easy. The pills arrived in a padded envelope with a Tennessee stamp. *Two to be taken both morning and evening on two consecutive days. No alcohol, aspirin, or strenuous exercise until the bleeding stops. In case of excessive blood loss or severe light-headedness seek medical advice immediately.*

Danny left messages twice a day to see if I had taken them yet. For a week I saw more of him than during the entire eight weeks that we'd been dating. Twice he made breakfast that I threw up into the kitchen sink. As the end of our easy-way-out window approached, I finally told him that I'd flushed all eight pills down the toilet, together with that morning's acid phlegm and tears.

He left without a word, and never called since.

⟨⟨⟨

A parasite can indirectly reduce the host's fitness further through various modes of pathology, ranging from causing changes in the host's behaviour, to acting as a vector for third-party pathogens.

On the night you decided to show your face, the streets were so badly covered in black ice that the buses didn't run. The taxi rank was deserted, so no one saw when the flood of amniotic fluid spilled down the inside of my thighs. The rapid onset of the fever took me by surprise. By the time I made it to the hospital, I was consumed by the shakes. Between contractions, the kindly nurse explained the various hormones and antibiotics she fed into my vein, to control the dilation and against the infection.

Just before sunrise the room suddenly filled with people. Lab coats, latex gloves, monitors, bleeping apparatus on wheeled metal frames. Two final puffs, a gush of warm jelly and fluid, then a glimpse of blue limbs, flaccidly dangling from the midwife's hands. They cut the cord as swiftly as a piece of cotton string, and before I even heard a cry, they whisked you away.

⟨⟨⟨

For almost two hours now, I've been staring at the hospital wall. There's only me, my own battered body, my own bewildered mind. For the first time in nine months, I am alone.

I'm free at last. I could just leave. Get up, pull on my clothes, flash a smile at the nurse's station, steal down the corridor and out into the street, back to the wretched flat, its dirty kitchen and my unmade bed. I'd lock the door and pull the curtains, take time to lick my wounds, order my thoughts, straighten out the mess. Get back to life, to people, to study. Pick up where I left off.

Why do I feel nothing but empty?

Some parasite-host relationships endure over the entire natural lifespan of the host. Inter-generational host-parasite coevolution occurs when both organisms continually adapt to one another.

Finally, they bring you back, cleaned, and neatly wrapped. Your candy mouth is somewhat parted, your brow relaxed. I touch your velvet scalp and your marzipan hands, and the plastic-taped cannula that must stay in your arm for the next couple of days.

'We'll give precautionary antibiotics for a while,' the midwife says, 'but all the tests are showing up fine.'

I look down on your sleeping body and think how exhausted you must be, having been thrown head-first into the chaos of the outside world. *My* chaotic world, *my* confusion, *your* inherited mess. I look at you and think I've never seen anything so tiny. So perfect. So complete.

Outside the milky hospital window, a pale winter sun rises over tired roof-top chimneys, trying its best to cheer up a newborn morning. Gently, I push both my hands under your bottom and head, lift your tiny body out of the sheets and slide you into the collar of my nightdress. Skin to skin, chest to chest, your sweet-smelling scalp under my chin. Your body takes on the shape to fit mine, and your shallow breaths tickle the nape of my neck.

Home
for the
Rising Sun

*Devon
Borkowski*

For the first day and a half he could pretend he hadn't noticed it starting. Like the itchy, borrowed knowledge in the back of his brain that cows lie down before a rainstorm – like Fern always said, don't want to know it'll rain? Don't look at the cows.

He kept the car radio low on those rare occasions he still had to drive, stopped wearing headphones on the subway, and started wearing them to stock shelves at work, the jack hanging loose, wire pulled through the belt loop on his jeans. And if Fern followed a little closer behind, if her put-on breathing seemed just over his shoulder? Well. Don't look at her either.

At a certain point, though, there's no stopping the weather.

'There is, a house, in New Or–'

He hooked his headphones over his ears, hiked his pants up as he walked. He kept his face turned to the road until the street player and his guitar were well out of earshot, past a Rite Aid, a Five Below, and the Tavern on Stokes. The bar was tempting, but the jukebox whir he could hear passing the door kept his feet carrying on – *'they called, the rising–'*

The corner ahead was choked off with foot traffic, and a cyclist squatting in the bike lane. The red lit walk sign held them all in place. Fern stood in the centre of the little clump of bodies, between a baby carriage and two boys carrying penny boards. She was dressed for the last time he took her dancing. Red lipstick, sleek green gown and pearl lined cleavage. Her hair played to its own private, muted breeze.

He ducked around the far side, stepping down off the sidewalk and clipping his hip on the cyclist's gear shift as he brushed by. He didn't give the light time to change, facing the intersection with a flat "don't try me" stare. The laid-on car horns and cursing had a twang to them, almost the pick up of a guitar riff. *'And God, I know, I'm one–'*

He thought about going home. Lying down in bed with the lights off, hitting his pen until the edges of the world dulled, and finishing off the bottle of Pink Whitney stashed beneath his mattress. But there was his mother to think of. His sister. And the little guy, too. He wouldn't bring this on them again.

Two blocks down and a left turn brought him to the parking deck. This early in the afternoon it sat vacant. Just him and Fern – barefoot now, and in sleepwear. Her eyes were backlit, gleaming out of every shadow.

His mother's car was on the second level, a Honda from the '90s. She'd bought it used four years back, trying to cut down on Lyft fees, and time spent walking alone at night. He pulled up the family chat. Taking the car for a road trip. He waited until the screen read **Delivered**, then set cellular status to **off**. His sister would be pissed. His mother... was better not to think on. They'd both have four days to come around towards forgiveness.

The spare key was taped behind the front licence plate. He dropped his useless phone into the cupholder, backed carefully out of the space. Driving never seemed to get any easier. He figured it was just one of those things that had to be taught young. Otherwise you spend the rest of your life approaching it with the strained intentionality of a new language.

He didn't touch the radio dials. Not even when the song started up, faint and full of static.

'My father was a gamblin' man, down in New Orleans'

···

Ten miles down 206 the static had all but bled out. The volume, to contrast, had grown with every turn of the tires. It was loud enough now that he was catching glares at stoplights. He kept his chin high, levelled back a long look through his lashes. Still, his top lip was starting to chap where he'd been worrying it with his teeth. His palms left sweat prints on the wheel. City driving was hard, sure, but at least it wasn't personal.

There was something sheltering about a city skyline, the way the buildings came up to cradle the street. A veritable fortress. The cosy crunch of urban infrastructure had fallen away over an hour ago, replaced by rolling yellow pastures, and far too much sky.

The people, too, kept him on edge. This far into hick country he stuck out, an outlier in the land of white farmers and white housewives.

He turned on Powell, side street cramped as ever. The radio calmed just enough to hear gravel grinding as he hugged the curb too tight. He pulled into the shoulder and rocked to a stop.

It was an empty stretch of bleached grey asphalt lined on either side by wheat. Wind rippled across the swaying yellow sea. There was the telephone pole – wrapped in wilted pink ribbons, a bedraggled teddy bear still tied below its limp, weather-beaten arms. And there, toeing the cracked pavement edge, was Fern.

If she'd had her thumb out she'd have looked like any other hitchhiker. Her wind-teased, tangled copper hair, black flannel tied above her midriff, bralette peeking through undone buttons. Her jeans rode low on her hips. They were torn out at the knees, and rolled to cuffs above the pull straps of her cowboy boots.

She still wore her dorm key. It hung from a cord around her neck. He watched her through the windshield, the glint of a bronzy key blade flashing as she pretended to breathe.

He stretched over the centre console and popped the passenger lock.

'I'm not your fucking valet, alright? You can get your own door.'

He held his breath, she held his gaze. Eric Burdon still crooning on the radio was the only thing not in stalemate.

Then the radio crackled. The song skipped, restarted with a buzzing mechanical whine. Fern was in the passenger seat. Her back was a bowstring line, her hands sat stiff on her thighs, above the torn edge of denim. A constellation of moles marked the knee closest to him, a coin-sized bruise blooming from the ball of it.

'You're early.'

He shifted the gear back to drive and pushed the gas pedal down. The radio volume raised just enough to be heard over the engine.

'It's not the anniversary,' she said, more obstinate now, 'you're early.'

'You started on your shit earlier this year.'

'Last year you were late.'

He bit hard on the inside of his cheek. Over the road ahead the sky was deepening to a rich, cornflower blue. March meant a 6 p.m. sunset. He pressed the gas a little harder: he wanted as many miles behind them as he could get before then.

'I don't understand why you're still angry.' Fern's voice permanently lay along a register of monotones. This one was low in her throat, somewhere around the range of *annoyed*, 'You're the one who made us late.'

'You came in my fucking house, Fee! Of course I'm pissed at you.'

She shrugged, or at least made a stiff approximation, 'I haunt you always. House, no house, what's the difference?'

'My siblings live there, man. It's different.'

The radio cut. He glanced towards her, and found her staring back.

'I would never hurt them.'

He believed that. Whether it was couldn't or wouldn't, she hadn't caused any real harm in the last six years. At least, not directly. Even so, hearing Fern's heralding song drift out from under his sister's bedroom door had twisted a knot in his stomach.

'Doesn't matter, I don't want you near them.'

'Well. Some things never change.'

A part of him really wanted to have that argument again. To give in to the pressing *what do you mean by that?* and let things devolve from there. Instead he spun the radio volume dial. Pointless as it was.

'Just play your music, Fee. Stop tryna start shit.'

❙❙· ❙❙❙❙· ❙❙·

It had been his favourite song once. Of course, Fern knew that. They'd only been about three months in, still tentative and mostly undefined when it first came up. She'd been on aux, legs swung over her dorm bed's headboard while she flicked through a "dad rock" playlist. It was hard to picture now, the way her eyes had lit up. He could remember loving that look, though. Half the things he'd confessed to her had been for the sheer enjoyment of watching her squirrel the knowledge away. The way she treasured each easy admission.

That the song now made him nauseous was undoubtedly why Fern picked it. She'd handled his heart carefully back then, but she knew how to twist a knife.

'There is, a house, in New Orleans,'

Fern swayed along. It looked less like dancing, and more like her head might be too heavy for her neck, lilting her from side to side.

'You can't possibly be enjoying this.'

The swaying paused, leaving her stuck with her neck at an odd angle, 'I like car rides.'

'I meant the song.'

'I don't know. I guess I don't really "*enjoy*" anything anymore.' She tipped her head the other way. Her hair brushed the centre console, 'It doesn't bother me though.'

The *not like it does you* was left implied.

They were on 295. Daylight had sunk from the sky, and the road was cast in blue. Traffic stayed sparse. He tried to be grateful for the easy drive.

Fern was starting to make herself comfortable, slouching in increments until she could tuck her knees against the dash. It was that way every year. The gradual loosening as they drove. In some ways he preferred the initial… wrongness. It kept him in the present.

He rolled his shoulders back, shaking out the tension, 'So, can we talk?'

'Uh oh.' She pursed her lip, 'I don't remember liking what comes after that.'

'Fee.' She smiled. Sort of. For a second, at least, he could see her teeth. 'We're gonna need to establish some ground rules on the music crap.'

Fern sunk further into her chair. She drew her knees up towards where her arms were folded across her chest. 'You tried to ignore me last year.'

Sometimes the years between twenty and twenty-six felt like lifetimes. Every year the gulf between their ages grew. He wondered when Fern would start to look like a child to him. He wondered who that would hurt more.

'Yeah, I know, and I'm sorry about that.' The radio popped. 'Honestly, I am!'

He stopped at a yellow, other cars rolled past them as they waited for it to turn red. He put his hand on the back of Fern's seat. She was pushing her tongue into the inside of her cheek, her face tight.

'I promise. I won't do it again.' He sighed, 'Just... you can't be starting a week early. It throws a lot of shit off for me.'

'What's your proposed solution?'

'Just go back to starting the day before. I'll get the message.'

'And if you decide to ignore me again?'

A honk from behind alerted him to the changed light. He flipped the car off as it swerved past them.

'You can trust me.'

The radio went static, and when the song came back on it was playing again from the beginning. *There is, a house, in New Orleans.* As far as he could tell, that was the closest Fern could get to a laugh.

'Maybe you should just focus on the road for a while.'

᎙ᎥᏒ ᎙ᎥᏒᎥᏒ ᎙ᎥᏒ

It was half past one in the morning when he blinked his eyes a second and woke up in the wrong lane.

'Motherfuck–'

A semi's horn blared as he yanked the wheel to the right. He was breathing hard, his heartbeat thrumming in his fingertips.

'Maybe you should start looking for a motel,' Fern said. She'd changed at some point into a band t-shirt – some DIY underground group she'd probably dragged him to basement shows for. Her key was now on a loop of yarn tied to her belt, and her Docs were on the dash.

'I'm fine.'

'Sure. I guess it would be kinda funny if we both died in car accidents.'

'Oh, are we calling yours an *accident* now?'

If she had a response for that he didn't catch it. He pressed his forehead to the steering wheel and let the air out through his teeth.

'You can't blame me for this forever.'

'Who says this is blame?'

He tightened his hands at ten and two, 'The fuck would you call it then?'

'Maybe it's love,' she said, chipping black flecks of polish from her nails, 'I loved you at one point, this could be what love looks like now.'

Somehow that was worse than blame. Fern shrugged, 'Or maybe it's just another terrible, tragic thing that happened, in a life already oversaturated with terrible tragedies.'

'Your life, or mine?'

'Both. Neither.'

'Fuck you.'

'I wish you had.'

The radio whined. He ran a hand down his face, pushing his bangs back from his eyes, 'Shit. Fee–'

'*–And it's been, the ruin, of many a poor boy,*' volume blasted up to thirty-five. Conversation over. He tried to sit up straight-er, to will the blurs of yellow and green in front of him into mile markers and headlight. The music had droned to white noise by that point, even the increased volume hadn't helped. He started scanning for any signs of an upcoming motel.

⫻⫻⫻

Fern ended up being the one to find it – noting the sign while he was busy pinching his thigh to stay alert. It was instinct to thank her with a pat on the knee, and he tried to hide the recoil when his palm met cold skin.

It was the Holly Motel. Holly Hotel would've sounded better, Fern pointed that out in the parking lot, but *hotels* were for people who don't pack boxes in department store stockrooms.

The clerk came out from a back office when they got to the front desk. She had eyebags under blonde bangs, and looked less than thrilled to be talking to him (and somehow even *less* thrilled when "House of the Rising Sun" started playing over the intercom), but she took his card without fuss. Fern followed the receptionist as she retrieved their key, trailing stiff fingers down her cheek. He wanted to tell her off, but there was no point. Not like the girl could feel it anyway.

They ended up in room seven. His phone speaker nearly blew out when he put the key in the door, so at least Fern found it funny.

The carpet felt a little grainy once he'd kicked his shoes and socks off. There was a framed print of a heron hanging above the double bed. He kept his t-shirt on but dropped the jeans, then lay down on top of the covers. Fern was floating a few feet down from the ceiling, lying back in the air to let her legs flutter.

'The front desk girl was pretty.'

He pushed up onto his elbows, 'Okay?'

'Didn't you think she was pretty?' He couldn't see her face, just her long hair dangling.

'Fucking- come on, Fee. Cut it out.'

It had been a long time since he'd looked with the intention of finding anyone pretty. With the last girl who'd loved him a permanent figment in his peripheral vision.

He took his phone out of his pocket, turned cellular back on and waited for the messages to come through. He could guess what most of them would say – Are you seeing things again? Are you drunk? Are you high? Is your head fucking cracked?

He checked the last received for each contact. From his mother it was, baby if you need help we can find another program. From his sister, slightly less gentle, I fucking can't with you. If you're dead I'll hate you forever. He shut it off again without responding to either.

He rolled over, buried his face into a scratchy pillow case and closed his eyes.

⫶⫶⫶

Another hour saw him lying on his back, hands crossed over his stomach. It was hard to see Fern beyond a dark shape drifting near the corner.

'Your note blamed me.'

His phone was on the nightstand. The song still played from it, but hardly any louder than the radiator. His eyes were starting to itch. Shutting them brought him no closer to sleep, though.

'What?'

'In the car you said you didn't blame me. Your note said otherwise.'

'I didn't see it that way.'

Whether she meant the conversation or the note she didn't specify.

'You know what I don't get?'

'Taxes.'

'What? No-'

'Therapy.'

'Stop it, no.' He brought his arms up over his face, 'Why would you write a note at all if you were going to do it as a car crash?'

Fern landed at the foot of his bed. The mattress didn't shift to accommodate her weight. He could see her a little better though, in the crack of street light coming through the blinds. Just a sliver of silver tracing the outline of her head.

'I'm not sure I understand the question.'

'I mean it would have looked like an accident, right? Without the note?' He pinched his lips together, 'Why not just... let it be that.'

She sat in perfect stillness for a while, considering. He found himself making his own breathing shallow to match the statue set of her shoulder.

'For closure, I think.'

He sat up, 'How was a letter supposed to give us closure?'

The speaker on his phone flared, popped like a gunshot. The song vibrated.

'Fuck- What?' He caught himself on the nightstand just short of tumbling out of bed.

Fern shrugged, 'It's funny. That's all.'

'What's funny?'

'How my whole life became, in an instant, just another bad thing that's happened to you.'

His hand drifted towards her, but he snatched it away before it reached.

'I didn't mean–'

'It was closure for me, not anyone else,' she said, 'I had things left to air out.'

'Is that why you're still... around, then? Still got something on your mind?'

Fern tipped back, disappearing over the lip of the bed, then buoyed up again toward the ceiling.

'Not right now. Maybe ask me again in the morning.'

〜 〜 〜

He woke to a full face of afternoon sun, and the sinking feeling they were going to be late for checkout.

He showered, which only made pulling on yesterday's jeans feel worse, and cursed his lack of foresight in not picking up a toothbrush. His whole mouth was fuzzy, and rubbing his teeth with a wet paper towel only went so far.

The woman at reception this time was older, mid-sixties, with a broad face and soft hands. He stuck his tongue out at Fern while she had her back to them. Fern made a show of pretending not to see.

There was only one other car still parked when they stepped outside, and it looked like they were also packing to go. A man struggling to fold down a double-seated stroller, and a boy with a bowl cut running laps around the car, mindful to step around the occupied baby carrier at his father's feet.

Icy fingers closed around the cuff of his jacket. Fern was watching the children with distant, pained eyes. The father was nearly mangling the stroller now, biting off curses under his breath. He looked back to Fern, then to the family again. He sighed.

'Need any help with that?'

The man looked wary, watching him approach, but he was used to that this far south. The man looked between his two kids and the awkwardly balanced stroller, and seemed to decide it was worth the risk.

'S'pose I could use the extra hands.'

He knelt down to look for the release button on the bottom seat.

'So what brings ya out to Knoxville?'

He popped the bottom seat loose and set it off to the side, then started on the adaptors. Fern was sitting cross legged in front of the baby carriage. She ran her pointer finger along the knuckles of his curled little fist. The baby's blueberry eyes were locked on her face. She sometimes had that effect on infants, like maybe they could see her too.

'A road trip. It's an annual thing.'

'My boys and I are on a road trip ourselves.'

Fern was making noises for the child now, a sort of melodic cooing. It took him a second to realise she was trying to hum, vaguely in the tune of "You Are My Sunshine".

He stood and lifted the stroller's folding joint, then flipped the locks around the frame. He pushed it over for inspection. Fern, seeing the job was done, leaned down to press her face to the baby's forehead. She held there for a moment before standing to go.

'I really appreciate the help.'

'No problem, man. Have a good one.'

Fern followed him back to the car without complaint. He opened the passenger door for her and pretended to be checking his glove compartment as she climbed in.

'Got your baby fix for the rest of the drive?' he said, trying not to look at her. Fern had always been so good with kids. She would've made a good mom. They'd talked a lot about it at the time, how different they'd be from their own parents, how ready they'd always been for the tantrums and the bad days.

He turned the key in the ignition and left the motel parking lot behind.

᛫ᛁᚠ᛫ ᛫ᛁᚠᛁᚠ᛫ ᛫ᛁᚠ᛫

As soon as her mood improved, Fern started whining about breakfast. He wanted to refuse on principle – *you don't actually eat, Fee*, but the rumbling of his own stomach forced capitulation. He went through the drive through at a Culver's. He ordered chicken fingers, and fries, which he put in the passenger cup holder for Fern to sniff at.

She was fully lounging in her seat – elbow propped on the centre console, one foot on the upholstery. He rolled down the window so she could hang out her other leg. With anyone else he'd have worried about it catching on something, but that wasn't really an issue for Fern.

'I'm pretty sure you're not supposed to sit like that in a dress.'

'No one can see me but you, what does it matter?'

'Maybe I don't want to see your panties either. Ever think of that?'

'Prude.'

She was in a red cotton scrap that could generously be called a sundress, and a decidedly familiar lightweight bomber.

'That's not your jacket.'

Fern shrugged, 'You threw it out when I died. It might as well be now.'

She sniffed at her fries again, touched one to the tip of her tongue. By the face she pulled, it wasn't as satisfying as she'd hoped.

'Do you remember the chicken fingers we got when we drove to PA?'

'Oh my god,' he laughed, 'that was somehow the best chicken I've had in my life.'

The radio crackled, Fern tipped her head back with a smile, 'Fucking PA chicken.'

'And I wasn't even high!'

'I would've killed you if you were.'

He merged into the left lane, cool air from the open window fluttering through his hair. 'I wasn't about to smoke before meeting your sister. Give me some credit.'

'My friends always said I gave you far too much.'

There was the echo of a sting there, dulled by a lack of surprise. He remembered their old dorm parties, sitting at Fern's desk chair with her in his lap, trailing his fingers over her sides and catching her around the middle when she doubled over laughing. The way her friends would politely avoid eye contact, then tactfully cap his drinks at two. He didn't go to the funeral. He figured the only person there who might've ever actually wanted him around was already ash in an urn.

⫻⫻⫻

He parked on North Rampart Street and walked to the cemetery. The trees they passed along the way were hung with thousands of strung plastic beads. It was just past four when they reached the wrought iron gates, the cemetery closed for the night. The filigree was easy for his sneakers to find purchase on as he boosted himself up and over. He nearly rolled an ankle, though, dropping off the other side.

Fern watched with a smile, arms crossed over her chest. While he was dusting grave dirt from the knees of his jeans she stepped up to the gate and put her hand to the metal. With a squeal, they swung open. She stepped inside.

'The fuck, Fee!'

She turned her palms up, 'It's like I've got a house key, I guess. It wouldn't have worked for you.'

They walked, winding through the raised tombs. Bodies were buried above ground here, Fern told him once, to keep the coffins from floating. She of course didn't have a real grave. Dust to dust and all that.

'If your ashes sorta blew away, why is this your... resting place?'

She pursed her lips and hummed, 'Maybe they didn't get very far.'

Their jackets brushed, hers still rustled like real fabric moving against his.

'Did you want it to be this graveyard?'

'I just asked to be brought to New Orleans in the note,' she said, 'I don't know who had to actually pick the place.'

'If you *had* picked?'

'Scattered over the Mardi Gras parade, for sure.'

He snickered, 'For sure.'

She led them over to one of the tombs. Marie Laveau, according to the plaque, which sat in stone above a planting urn of blue flowers. The stone was scratched in x marks, clustered in threes. He sat with his back to the grave and Fern sat down in front of him, the curve of her spine between his shins. She was warm, her ribs expanding with each breath. He spread his legs and let her slot herself between them. Her back to his chest, head tucked under his chin.

'She was called the Voodoo Queen.'

'Hmm?'

Fern gestured absently behind them, grazing his cheek in the process, 'The woman buried here. They say she can still grant wishes. It was on my list of things to see when we came together.'

He wrapped his arms around her and squeezed. Her hands settled over his. There were so many places he'd promised to take her. New Orleans was the big one, of course, but then there'd been the beach (his promise on the worst of her bad days. *Don't be like that – I'll take you to the beach! Who could be sad at the beach?*), and the Met, and one nearly blackout drunk vow to take her little sister to Disney World. He ducked his chin, buried his face in the crown of her hair.

'I never wanted to hurt you, Fee.'

'Oh. But you were so good at it.'

His eyes felt tight. He squeezed them shut, breathed through his nose. One hand slotted just under Fern's jaw. The other, around her waist, she intertwined her fingers with, and ran her thumb over the back in soft circles. She leaned into the hand around her neck.

'Why did you leave me?'

He kissed the side of her head, let his mouth linger, 'Could ask you the same question.'

'You left first.'

'I had a lot going on... it was complicated.' A laugh heaved out of him, and the damn behind his eyes cracked, 'I thought you'd be better off.'

She reached up to run her knuckles below his lashes.

'I wasn't.'

'Yeah, I get that *now!*'

He bowed over her, absorbing her body into his as he shook. He was too tired to be embarrassed to cry. She moulded into his hold, locked her arms over his, shushing and soothing and letting him pull her close. His mouth was over her forehead now, dark hair tickling her face, but she made no move to push him away.

'It's not my fault. It's not my fucking fault.'

'I know,' she said, 'I never meant it to be.'

'I didn't fucking kill you, Fee.'

'I know.'

She turned into the hand on her jaw and kissed the palm. Her warm, dry mouth against his calluses. Then she took the one from her stomach, where their fingers were linked, and kissed the back. She pet at the nape of his neck, and trailed fingers over his arms until he felt like he could breathe again.

When all but the trembling had subsided, she pointed to the horizon, just visible through backlit monoliths. Pink clouds were drifting over the setting sun.

'My mom used to call that the sun's pink blanket,' she said. 'When I was really little, she'd pretend the sun was tucking itself in for bed.'

'You must miss her.' His throat was raw.

Fern rubbed her thumb across the ball of his wrist.

'Yes. It seems I do.'

'I'm sorry.'

'That's not your fault either.'

Her head lolled onto his shoulder. She turned in, kissed his clavicle.

'I think it's almost time.'

The phone speaker hummed, nearly mournful, *oh mothers, tell your children, not to do what I have done*. He kissed her forehead, then her crown. He held her as close as he could. When the sun slipped below the sea of graves she whispered his name against the back of his hand, and was gone.

'See you soon.' He would. It was never very long before she started to pop up again. A head of copper hair in a crowd, the flash of a green dress, the figment drifting closer and closer across the year.

His knees popped as he stood, stretching his back experimentally. He gave a pat to Ms. Laveau's tomb. It crossed his mind to leave behind an x or three of his own, to ask for a wish, but he couldn't think of anything worth wishing for. Not anything a dead woman could do for him, anyway. He started the walk back towards his car. It would be a long drive. Longer still without the radio, his ears ringing in the silence.

Happy Seedful Day

Deborah Zafer

Seedful Day arrives as it always does, but this year, it is my turn.

Two years ago, my sister Vida chose an apple. It was small and withered but when they cut it open it had six seeds and so she was called blessed and is now engaged to Eran the bank teller's son who will, they say, grow into a fine young man. Mama is very happy and on Fridays, she cuts Vida an extra large piece of pie, touches her arm and smiles. Only I know that Vida thought she was choosing a tomato and so when Mama serves tomatoes now, we laugh to ourselves, and always will.

I think Vida is happy. If she wasn't she would have told me. So far, she has said nothing at all and we have carried on talking as usual about our friends and our animals and what we will eat for lunch or dinner. Papa's nickname for Vida is Little Locust. He jokes that with her appetite, she could strip a field bare in seconds.

Seven years ago, my sister Elena chose the orange and now she is married to Luca the builder's son. They have two sons and one more on the way. Elena's husband buys her beautiful clothes to wear on visit days. Her neck is heavy with jewellery and whenever she looks at her sons she smiles. So, from this, the village knows my family are good people and blessed and Mama can hold her head high in the market and anywhere else she chooses to go.

'That is all good for you,' Mama says as she brushes my hair at night, her knees tucked up behind me. 'For me, it was harder because of your aunt Riva who picked a tomato and then produced nothing from her womb. Who knows why? For this, they called us cursed and this is the reason only your father would marry me.'

Mama says no more but I know what she means. Papa's father was known as a drunk with a mean spirit and the apple has not, I think, fallen far from the tree. I don't have a nickname for Papa, but if I did, it would not be one I would say out loud.

I hold Mama's hand.

'I am blessed,' I say, 'thank you.'

One year ago, my friends and I were taken after school to the village hall, blindfolded and given the gloves to try on. Vida had told me how thick they were but when I put them on, I was still surprised at how hard it was to feel anything through them. I put my hand to my face, my heart, and felt nothing at all.

'The *only* way to know is from the size and the weight,' Renata the priest's wife told us, her voice thick with emotion, as we felt around in our baskets blindly. 'You must practise at home until you know the heaviness, the girth, the give of the fruits, especially the potato. You don't want to pick a potato and end up like Mara.'

'No!' the girls squealed together. No one wanted to end up like that.

Mara lived in the house at the end of our village. Alone. Many people said that she was a witch, or something like it. Once Vida and I walked past to try and see her. The trees were overgrown, the flowers wild. At first, we saw nothing and soon Vida with her restless spirit grew bored and wandered off to play with the others in the field. I stayed. Mama had gone out for the day to visit my poor aunt and I remember the sense of peace that came from knowing no one awaited me or needed anything from me. Many minutes, or maybe hours later Mara emerged to peg her washing, a cat by her feet, singing. She did not look frightening at all. In fact, if anything, it was her happiness that scared me and caused me to run away and never look back.

Later, when Vida asked me what I saw, I told her I saw nothing. Nothing at all.

For the rest of the year, Mama and Vida helped me to practise after school. The pomegranate had the most seeds and was the one to aim for. It was bumpy and medium-heavy, deceptively light when you think of how many seeds it could hold. The next best was the orange or tomato and then the apple and avocado. Everything was OK except the potato which, we were told, would consign you to a life of solitude. One by one my mama and sister placed them in my hands, which they had wrapped in layers of wool. My small sisters watched anxiously from the sidelines.

'This?' they would ask, 'and now this?' I always got it right.

Sometimes on our way to school, the boys would call to us. My best friend Marisol was beautiful with big breasts and so often a boy would shout something like, 'Hey Mari, pick a pomegranate for me,' and she would put her head down and only I would know that really, she was thinking of how, if she chose a pomegranate, she could end up marrying Ezra the mayor's son, and this was what Marisol wanted more than anything. I knew that and she knew I knew that but we never spoke of it and in fact, still spoke as if we were girls with all the choices in the world.

No boys ever called to me. Not once. Whether that was because Marisol's shadow was so large or whether it was because they could tell my heart didn't yearn for them, who can say, but either way it wounded only my vanity and never my spirit.

One night when Mama and I were coming back from our swim and the sky was warm and dark like a cloak, I roused my courage to ask her, 'Mama, what if I don't want to marry and have children? What then?'

Mama stopped walking and knelt down next to me. 'What do you mean, ChuChu? What else is there?'

'I don't know,' I answered. And it was true, I didn't.

We continued walking home as if nothing had happened between us that was not ordinary.

Only in dreams did I allow myself to think of what there might be that was not what my mama had. Pale versions of my body darted in and out of view, trying to climb mountains that grew ever taller or horizons that kept moving further and further away. Once I was a school teacher with rows and rows of girls facing me, all with the face of Vida tilted upwards and eager to learn.

'You were moaning in your sleep again, ChuChu,' Vida would say when I awoke to find the covers tangled all around my body and my heart in knots. There were two more years left for us to share the bed before she would move to her new family and then I would be left to dream alone. It was unimaginable for me to think of sleeping without her beside me.

On the day itself, Mama dresses me in a beautiful white dress with green seeds sown around the bottom and small red pomegranates around the collar. It is the dress that Mama, Vida and Elena wore before me and so it is blessed and imbued with good fortune.

Mama and Papa take my hands and we walk to the village hall. From every corner, I see my friends in their dresses and also the boys from the village flanked by their proud parents who will today be able to choose the right wife for their son. We walk along the well-trodden path, the same way I walk to school, and I feel like I know every flower and tree and bush and I nod to them all, wishing them good morning.

Mama's hand is firm and warm around mine. I know she is confident I will choose well because we have practised so often, and also because I come from a line of women known for fruitfulness and good sense.

When we arrive, Mama spies her friend Arina in the crowd wearing a bright hat like a blue butterfly and goes to her briefly to say hello. Their conversation must only last twenty or thirty seconds. At that moment, my papa bends down, mouth next to my ear so close his breath feels like fire and whispers 'you don't have to do it, you know, Channela? It isn't the only life there is.'

Then, as Mama returns, he stands back up and takes my hand as if nothing had happened. And maybe it hasn't.

As we walk in, I try to catch his eye but he looks straight ahead without even a flutter of his eyelids.

I consider my Mama and Papa as we sit in our chairs. The priest sings of life and love and fruitfulness and the community responds 'amen,' 'amen' and 'amen,' again as we have been taught to do from birth.

Are my parents happy? I have never thought of it before. Only that they have done what we are supposed to do and that they have raised us to do the same in the way of our community and our village and our Lord who asks nothing of us and gives so much.

But also, I think of my papa and the way he slips out the back door whenever he can, and sits upon the hillside smoking his pipe and looking out at the hills. And I realise for the first time that his, like mine, is a spirit that needs peace and that in our house, there is no peace, and therefore this might explain some of the things I like so little about him.

I don't ask myself if Mama is happy. Some things are too painful to explore.

'Now arise, daughters of the village,' says the priest and Mama places the veil upon my face so I cannot see and Papa puts the gloves upon my hands so I cannot feel and together they lead me to the front where my basket awaits.

Now have they grown and soon they will sow
Sweet are the fruits of the valley of our Lord
Once they were girls and now, they will know
That the path to the Lord is through fruitfulness
So now sing we all and together we pray
On this our happy Seedful Day

The congregation sing as they stand and sway. Beyond, I hear the women clapping and crying as they remember their own Day of Choosing and how they felt then, for better or worse. The men stamp their feet in rhythm and the voices of the young girls and boys rise high, overlaying them all in harmony. Oh, truly, it is a beautiful thing.

My papa squeezes my hand and moves back into the crowd. My mama pulls me close and whispers, 'choose well little bird.'

I am alone. Behind me is my childhood and in front, something else entirely.

My friends and I take our seats and wait for the priest to ring the bell. All of our lives we have waited for this moment to know what will become of us, who we will be.

The bell rings once. Twice.

I place my gloved hands into the basket and move them around, trying to feel.

As I do, I think of my papa sitting on the hill with his back to us, of my mother kindling the fire every night to keep us warm, of Marisol so ready for what awaits her, of my young sisters whose future depends on me choosing well and of Mara alone and singing. I feel them all with me as I try to work out what is what and what my role in it all is.

We can take as long as we want but we must all finish at the same time.

Some years the ceremony goes on for many hours and no one minds. In other years it is a matter of minutes.

Music plays in the background whilst we choose and the community hum along together like bees in a hive. The sound is so soothing that after a while I feel no nerves at all.

Next to me, I hear Marisol raise her head and whistle. She is done.

And on the other side, my neighbour does the same.

I have made my choice and, in my gloved hand, I hold my future. I know it by its heaviness, its circumference, and the way it feels.

I wait for them to remove my veil, to cut the fruit and find within whatever they will find. I hold my head high knowing surely now, from this moment on, I am blessed.

⫴ ⫴⫴ ⫴

It takes many years for Mama to talk to me again.

When I think back on the moments after I whistle, I see only confusion. I think I place my basket on the table before I run but I cannot be sure.

I think there is murmuring, maybe shouting. I think that maybe I see my papa rising to his feet. I think he points to the door.

All I know is that something takes hold of me and causes me to run and run and run and that as I run, I cast off the gloves and the veil and leave them on the floor of the hall. I hold only one thing in my hand and I keep that close to my chest.

I run far. I leave the paths I know well. I say goodbye to the flowers and trees and plants that have been my companions. As I run, I hear my breath ragged in my chest like a roar but I do not allow my legs to stop. There is no going back.

I do not allow myself to think of Vida or of my small sisters.

When I get to the house, the door is closed but I bang and bang until it opens and Mara stands there, surprised. She does not walk among us so she does not know me.

I hold out my hands for her to see. A large potato nestles in my palm, like a pup.

We stand there silently as she looks at it and at me.

'You'd better come in,' she says finally, standing back and allowing me to enter her house.

It is bigger than it looks from the outside and I feel like we walk down many different, darkly-lit passageways until eventually we reach the hearth, upon which a pot boils.

She motions to me to sit down in a chair next to the fire.

'Are you sure of what you are doing?' she asks, sitting down opposite me. 'Do you understand?'

'I do,' I say, 'I know I cannot do what they want me to do. Not now. Maybe never.'

'That is understandable,' she says and holds out her hand to me, 'to me, at least. Maybe not to many.'

I nod at her and put the potato into her hand. She takes it to her worktop where she peels and dices it and then, together, we drop the pieces into the pot where they join the other vegetables and a small joint of meat.

It is a funny thing but that evening seems to go on for a very long time until suddenly it is morning and I wake up in a bedroom that feels like it was made just for me, so perfectly do its dimensions and contents suit me.

I am also certain that on that first morning and every time I leave the house I do so by a different passageway. I definitely never take the same route twice.

I weigh in my mind what the people in my village have said about Mara being a witch, and find that I neither know if it is true or false and that I do not care, for she keeps me safe and asks nothing of me but that my ways are pleasant when we meet one another.

Every year after then, even until this very day, another girl arrives bringing us another potato to add to the pot.

In our house, Seedful Day becomes known as Día de la Papa and over time we develop our own rituals that start to draw interest from wider than the village. We make potato pancakes and eat them in the garden, sprinkled with paprika and salt, and we dance and sing.

Sometimes visitors come and once I saw a mother holding up a small girl wearing a dress embroidered with the leaves of the potato plant. It is not a thing I thought to see.

If sometimes there are other visitors who shout and chant words that are less friendly, it is best not to think of them.

'They are afraid, that is all,' Mara says to us as she closes the curtains and stokes the fire.

After a few years, boys start to come too. I always think we will run out of space, but we never do. There is room for all.

Occasionally, I see Vida in the village, but she does not raise her head. I think it is because her husband Eran has told her not to. This is what I have to think in order to survive.

Mama comes to me only once. She brings with her a basket of fruits and places it in front of me.

'Happy Seedful Day, ChuChu,' she says, her eyes cast down.

'Thank you, Mama,' I say, and I take a knife and cut the fruits open so that we can eat together.

She speaks little but she does not have to for when she raises her eyes they are heavy with love and also, I think, with feeling that is somewhere between pride and jealousy and sadness and anger. With all of these things together.

When she goes, she puts her hand to my face and says, 'do not forget, Little Bird, that sweet are the fruits of the valley of the Lord. There is always a way back to the right path.'

'Thank you, Mama,' I say, holding on to her hand briefly and then letting it fall, 'I will think on it.'

I watch her walk away and then, with the fruits still sweet in my mouth, I go back into the house where I am sucked back into my new world with its many corridors, unsure where I will end up, but free, at last, to choose.

Acid

Claire Beaver

Sydney had recently gotten very into citrus. She loved the way it smelled, the vast variety of lemons, limes, oranges, grapefruits, pomelos, yuzus. The pores of their rough skin in her palm reminded her of her own eczemaed arms. Sydney couldn't wait to try them all, to shrivel her tongue to nothing with the acid of sweet and bitter juices dripping freely down her chin, drying in a sticky trail. Vibrant yellow, soft pink, sensual shades of greens and oranges, revealing the fleshy insides, perfectly separated by a translucent border of skin that may or may not match the colour advertised on the outside; it was divine.

Today, Sydney was going to try a kumquat. *Citrus japonica.* She'd heard you didn't even need to peel them, just pop the entire fruit in your mouth and chew. She spent hours on the internet, researching the *Rutaceae* family, imagining all the genera and species she could fill her plastic bowls with. Always clear bowls, so she could see the colours of each adventure. Her eyes burned by the time she decided on the humble kumquat as her next exploration; she was between that and the *Calamansi*, colloquially the Philippine lime, but liked the fact that the kumquat was small. Consumed in one mashing of the jaw.

Sydney plugged in her laptop and got dressed, a plain grey sweater from her closet and the jeans she peeled off her floor. There were clothes all over her apartment, hanging on the back of her desk chair where she did her research, shoved under her bed, pushed into corners. She would get around to washing them; for now, she was only concerned about the kitchen on the other side of her studio apartment, where the blue mosaic backsplash shone bright and the countertops had not a crumb. This was where she kept her fruit.

She stepped over the piles of clothes and stacks of books and tangled wired headphones to get to the dining room table, or the small IKEA table that had two stools beneath it; her mom had insisted she get a space to eat that was not her bed. It was also littered with things; crusty forks, bowls with liquid dried in their bottoms, credit card bills and letters she never answered. She had a quill and ink set on the window sill that she had used vigorously until she found her passion for roller skating, the likes of which were now somewhere beneath the clothes with scuffed black knee pads shoved inside them. She had some knitting needles and yarn crumpled on top of the highest pile of books she'd never gotten around to reading, and her toolbox sat open next to the old VHS player she'd intended to fix. She had scoured pawn shops for those for weeks, even settling for DVD players, so she could resell them and make some money. It was going well, until she found what she really cared about. Citrus. She needed to get to the store. She grabbed the keys to her car and her phone from beneath a letter from Mountain State Community College advertising summer classes and closed the door behind her, not bothering to turn off the lights. She raced down the stairwell.

Sydney imagined each stop light colour as a different variety of fruit, a red grapefruit, a Meyer lemon, a Kaffir lime. The Kaffir lime was one of her favourites, its thick skin rough like a brain. She smiled at the thought of her very first taste.

Suddenly a sound blared from her jeans, alerting her of an intruder. She fished for it while trying to keep her eyes on Division Street. West Virginia drivers were not known for paying attention, and this old car had too many miles on it for her to trust it fully. She knew who was calling before she answered; there were only two people who called, and her therapist wasn't scheduled until Thursday.

'Hi Sydney,' the voice crackled. Her phone was on its way out.

'Hi Mom,' Sydney answered, her phone held by her shoulder against her ear. She tightened her grip on the steering wheel.

'Are you driving?'

'Yes.'

'Are you going to work?'

'Yes.' Sydney's mother would never understand what she was actually heading towards. She didn't understand joy for its own sake.

'Early shift. Make sure you eat something.'

'I will.'

'Did you take your vitamins?'

'Yes.'

'You need to take that with food,' her mother added.

'I know.' Sydney flicked her blinker.

'Are you lying?'

'No.' She didn't understand why she was always asked this. Even if she was, her mother should trust her.

'Okay. I'm going out to Duck to see Grandpa. Aunt Sissy is there already, but the nurse said he's been asking about us.'

'Okay.'

'Can you come after your shift?'

Sydney drove past the Sonic she told her mother she worked at. When she moved into Parkersburg, she had to have a job that she could pay her own rent with and that would keep her to a schedule, that was the deal. She had one, it just wasn't that one.

'I don't think I'll have time. Working a double today. I'll call you later, though.'

'Sydney, I think this is important. You really can't make it?'

'No,' Sydney said. 'I'm really busy here.' Sydney tried suppressing her irritation; she was 27 years old. She could make decisions for herself. Her grandpa barely spoke anyway.

'Okay, well please try and make it over if you can.' A pause. 'Have a good day at work.'

'Thanks, Mom. Bye.' She hung up just as she was pulling into the parking lot behind the McDonald's. If she did want a job in fast food, there was no short supply of potential employers. But she didn't. She got her favourite spot, just next to the doors.

It was 6:53AM. Kroger opened at 7. Sydney was buzzing, thinking of what lay in store for her. She was glad she hadn't slept. Her adrenaline forced her out of the car and to the automatic doors where she waited for a teen employee to come and let her in. She paced, hugging her arms to her chest to try and calm herself down but she couldn't help that she was just so excited to get in there and get what she had come for.

Finally a pimply girl about 4 feet high came over to the sliding doors. She twisted the lock slowly, rolling her eyes at Sydney, who stood just on the other side of the clear glass. It had barely begun to slide open when Sydney squeezed through. She had a mission, and Aisle One was where her journey would finally begin. She saw the wilting leaves getting their first showers of the day, bruised peaches and plums, tomatoes looking mealy even from the outside, bananas already speckled with brown spots. Then she arrived at the citrus. Lemons, then limes, then oranges. She knew a Meyer lemon from a Eureka lemon, even if the workers did not as they were all stacked under the neon yellow label. As if all lemons were the same.

Her eyes finally met the sign for tropical fruits. Sydney scanned quickly. Where were the kumquats? She grew frantic, scanning again and again. Half of these weren't even tropical, just fruits that the people in West Virginia wouldn't see on the trees in their backyards. Why were the onions here? Sydney's vision began to blur. She needed to find someone fast. She began pulling at her cuticles as she raced up and down each aisle until finally she spotted an older lady opening the register.

'Excuse me!' Sydney said.

The lady jumped a foot, higher than Sydney would ever have thought her body could go. 'Oh lord, girl, you scared me so bad,' the lady said as she clutched her heart next to a name tag that read June.

'I'm sorry,' Sydney replied. 'I don't see the kumquats and I need to find them.'

'Cucumbers?' the lady replied, smoothing back her brown hair splashed with grey streaks.

'Kumquats.' Sydney was trying not to raise her voice.

'Hmm,' she said, obviously trying to use her brain.

'You do or you don't know?' Sydney demanded.

'I'll ring Camel and see if he knows,' she said, then ever so slowly pressed the intercom button. 'Camel, can you come up to register three? A girl needs help.'

Sydney ran her sweaty palms down her thighs, trying to dry them. She resumed picking until Camel, a bald beanpole of a man whose age was indeterminable, came over. 'Morning, June.'

'Hey Camel,' June smiled at him.

Jesus Christ, Sydney thought.

'Do you know where the cucumbers are?'

'Kumquats,' Sydney corrected. Looking at Camel meant looking at his blue apron, not his eyes. She didn't care to look up.

'Kumquats. Yeah, Aisle One.'

'I was there already, I didn't see them.'

'Let's check it out,' Camel said. He motioned for Sydney to follow him and made his way back to Aisle One. She followed closely behind. Her finger was bleeding where she'd peeled her skin off. It didn't matter.

Camel looked up and down the produce section as slowly as Sydney believed a person could. Then he turned towards the displays in the middle of the aisle. There were packets of seeds filling up a bucket in one section, with plastic shovels hanging off the sides. The next was filled with three kinds of apple; red, yellow, green.

'There you go,' Camel said, using his long arm to point at the very first display at the front of the aisle. How had she rushed past it? 'Those are pretty good, I tried 'em for the first time yesterday, actually. I like regular old oranges better, but the manager says these are popular now.'

Sydney grabbed a bag. Crinkling cellophane holding what had consumed her mind. She felt saliva well up beneath her tongue as she looked at them. She rushed back to the registers, leaving Camel behind. She didn't see anybody standing where they should be. 'Is anyone here?' June came out from behind some door over to the side of the store.

'Sorry, sweetie, just had to pee there,' she said. She waddled over to her post and scanned the card that hung around her neck. The cash drawer popped open, she closed it, and finally she turned to Sydney. 'Just that, then?'

Sydney gave a tight smile. She feared what might come out if she spoke.

'Have a good day.' June said after slowly sliding the precious fruit over her grimy counter and taking Sydney's cash.

Sydney ran through the parking lot, taking a deep breath when she was back in the driver's seat of the old Impala. She clamped her arm around her mouth and screamed. Then she put her car in reverse and drove home, her goods placed on the front seat where she could see them.

Sydney carried her kumquats up the stairs and into her apartment as fast as she could. She needed to shower. To keep her fruit comfortable, she grabbed a smaller bowl from her cupboard and placed it on the counter. She took each tiny oval out of the bag and gave it a little rinse in the sink. She then gingerly dried them off with a paper towel and placed them one by one into her bowl. She thought they would be happiest next to the bowl of navel oranges, a bigger cousin of sorts.

Her phone began to sing again, and she pulled it out to hit decline. Didn't her mother know she was at work? She stripped off her clothes, dropping them on the floor on her way to the bathroom.

Light shone through the small window, throwing slashes of white across her body. She had her shower scalding hot, letting her long black hair slide down her back in a slick waterfall. She closed her eyes and tried to imagine what her first bite would taste like. She did this always, getting herself clean and ready so it could just be her and her senses and the citrus. Sydney faced the water and let her mouth fill with it, gargled and spit it out. She needed to have a neutral palate and didn't want toothpaste marring the taste. She knew what that was like with orange juice, and this experience would be in an entirely different category than her childhood breakfasts where her parents insisted she needed more vitamin C. After quickly scrubbing her scalp with shampoo, she got out and dried herself off. She looked at herself in the mirror above the line of serums that hadn't been touched in months. She was finally ready.

Sydney closed all the blinds in her apartment and shed the purple towel she'd wrapped around herself. It was early afternoon but she needed to block out all distractions, anything that could interrupt. She laid her towel out on the floor next to her bed, where she'd pushed some things aside. She grabbed the bowl and placed it directly in front of her. She took a deep breath.

The kumquat was firm but not hard. Ripe. She rolled it between her fingers to release the aromatic oils, just as she had read on the internet. This would prep the fruit, allow its orange skin to connect with hers. She rolled it and rolled it, rubbing it up and down her arms. Then, she popped the small fruit in her mouth and bit down. The sweetness of the peel greeted her taste buds. The smoothness of the skin met the scent left behind and filled her senses marvellously. The kumquat burst its sour juice on her tongue as she bit through the rind. She squeezed her eyes shut even tighter at the sensation; it was heavenly. It was like she was eating and drinking at the same time; two essential human needs rolled into a citrus fit snug in the palm of her hand. She was surprised at the sour tang of the juice, but not negatively. She enjoyed that she didn't know exactly what to expect. She fished a seed from the segments of flesh in the membrane, holding it beneath her tongue as she chewed up the rest of the fruit. She spat the seed into the palm of her hand once she had swallowed. The kumquat had astonished her.

Sydney opened her eyes. She placed the green seed next to her on her towel and selected a new kumquat. She first rolled it between her palms, each fruit deserving to release all of their natural talents, then pierced it with her nail and tore it open, now ready to look at its insides. Five segments separated by thin membrane, with the pith in the centre; a wheel of beauty created naturally from the branches of a small tree, just for her. This time she fished the seed out with her nail before popping the halves in her mouth. She smiled as she chewed it up, taste buds rejoicing. She swallowed it and picked her bowl up. She placed it back on her counter, then grabbed a baby pink t-shirt that was on top of the roller skates against the wall next to her bed. She grabbed a pair of underwear from her drawer and slid them on, then opened her blinds to let the light in once again.

Sydney grabbed her phone from the dining table and unplugged her laptop, still reeling. She plopped on her bed and saw three more missed calls from her mother, along with a text that read please call me back sydney! How urgent could it possibly be? She would call her back after work. She opened her laptop and went incognito mode to **camsxx.com**. She logged into her account and opened her room.

She pulled her legs up on the bed and sat cross-legged, looking at bowls of citrus just across the room. She ran her fingers through her hair, hoping today there would be more customers looking for the girlfriend-type emotional fulfilment than for physical asks. She was in the mood to chat; she was feeling vulnerable and open. How could she possibly share the feelings she was experiencing with anyone else?

A message popped up on the right side of her screen: **greg173** has entered the room. 'Hi Greg,' Sydney said. She smiled at the camera.

greg173: hi

'How are you?' she asked him, fixing her hair a bit.

greg173: good. can u take ur shirt off

Sydney rolled her eyes. 'Don't you want to get to know each other first?'

greg173: I will tip u

Sydney adjusted herself, tucking her legs beneath her to sit on her feet. She noticed her phone ringing again and tried to ignore it. Another text from her mother popped up: it's grandpa, sydney pick up. She flipped her phone over and plastered her smile back on her face.

'I want to share something with you, if you want to see it,' Sydney said to her screen.

greg173: yes

'One second.' Sydney tilted her screen down and went over to her bowl. She carried it carefully back to her bed and set it down in her lap. She held up one of her perfect fruits to show to **greg173**.

'Do you know what this is?' she asked him.

greg173: no

'It's a kumquat. A little citrus fruit. It's amazing, I wish I could give you one.'

greg173: me 2

'Do you want to watch me eat it?' Sydney asked. She had never done this before on camera, shared so much of herself. Her inner self. 'It's really something special.' **greg173** said nothing. Sydney rolled the kumquat around in her hands and popped it into her mouth.

greg173: u don't peel it?

'No! You eat the whole thing, peel and all. You just have to spit out the seeds,' she said and spat the little green seed into her hand. She held it up to the camera.

greg173: eat more

'Oh, now you are interested, huh?'

greg173: kinda

Another person entered the room: **handsomeman1**.

handsomeman1: hey sexy

'Welcome, handsome,' Sydney said, already having selected her second fruit.

greg173: r u gonna eat more

handsomeman1: what is that

'It's a kumquat!' Sydney exclaimed.

greg173 tipped 11 tokens

greg173: eat another

'My pleasure.'

handsomeman1: wtf

handsomeman1 has left the room

Sydney popped the fruit directly into her mouth this time, forgoing the rubbing for immediate taste. She was laughing without even realising she was doing it.

greg173 tipped 5 tokens

Her phone lit up again. 'OH MY GOD,' Sydney exclaimed, pulled out of her moment.

greg173: why did u stop

She answered the phone. 'Mom. I am at work! What do you want from me?'

'Sydney, please come over here,' her mother said. Her voice was hoarse. 'I don't think grandpa will make it through the night, and you should say goodbye.'

'I can't, I'm working!'

'Sydney, this is your grandfather! Please just leave work, they will understand,' her mother screeched at her.

'No they won't!'

'How can you still act like this?'

'Grandpa won't even realise if I come so why drive all the way to Duck when I should be here making money?!'

greg173 has exited the room

'Shit!' Sydney said.

'Fine, don't come then,' her mom said in the quiet voice she reserved for when she was especially angry.

'I already said I can't!' Sydney was practically screaming now. She heard her mother breathing. Dial tone. Her mother had actually hung up on her. She flipped over and screamed into her pillow, shaking her bed. The bowl tipped over and her kumquats rolled all over her comforter and onto the floor.

'No, no, no, no,' Sydney said. She frantically tried to gather them all. She picked up a kumquat that had been caught by a hairball. She went to rub the dust off of it and noticed her shirt had caught little drops of water. She hadn't realised that she was crying.

She wiped her eyes viciously and scrambled around her dirty floor on her hands and knees for the rest of the fallen citrus. She gathered them all in her bowl after squeezing under her bed and searching through clothes. She held the bowl tight to her chest then rose to get them to the sink. She ran and turned the faucet on. Then she stopped and stared into her beautiful bowl of small orangey fruits, now speckled with dirt and dust and hair and crumbs. She threw the bowl into the middle of the room. She wiped more of her tears away and went back to her laptop. Sydney threw the covers over her head and curled into a ball, turning her laptop on its side to prop the blanket up in a little tent. She knew the only thing that could make her feel better was the *Calamansi*. The Philippine lime. She began to research.

The Autonomous Bicycle

Kurt Newton

It was late in the afternoon when the delivery truck arrived at the home of George and June Brimble. 'Honey, it's the bicycle!' George said, peering out the front window.

June was less enthusiastic. 'I would have thought it would have driven itself here.'

'Very funny,' said George. He hurried to the door leading to the garage. The backup beep of the delivery truck grew louder as the garage door rose. George greeted the driver as he exited the vehicle.

'Good day, sir. And how are you today?'

'Fine, thanks. Are you George Brimble?'

'Yes, I am.'

'Sign here, please.'

George signed the electronic signature plate. The driver then opened the twin doors on the back of the truck. Inside was a box larger than a television set but smaller than a refrigerator. The driver, a man of considerable heft and musculature, placed his rather large hands on either side of the box and easily slid it off the truck and onto the driveway. 'There you go,' he said. 'Enjoy.'

As the truck departed, George stared at the box and the possibilities within. His heart raced a bit. He then took a deep breath and dragged the box into the garage. It took most of his strength to do so, a perfect example as to why he had ordered the bicycle in the first place. George's body was not the athletic specimen it had been when he and June first married. But with the kids now grown and in pursuit of their own lives, George felt the need to do something wholly for the fun of it. And if it improved his health in the process – so the next time he dragged something heavy into the garage he wouldn't be so winded – so be it.

He cut the nylon straps, lifted the lid and peered inside.

'Is that it?'

George jumped. 'Jesus, woman, don't sneak up on me like that!' June had come to see what all the excitement was about. The bike appeared to be in sections: the main body, two wheels, a large cushioned seat and a pair of handlebars all set neatly in foam cut-outs. An instruction booklet sat on top of it all with the words **READ BEFORE ASSEMBLY** on the front cover. George closed the lid. 'Maybe I should do this after dinner,' he said. His wife turned then. 'It's your toy,' she said. 'Dinner will be ready in fifteen minutes.'

George opened the lid again. He grabbed the instruction booklet. As he thumbed through it this warning jumped out at him:

> **CRITICAL:** BICYCLE ASSEMBLY MUST BE
> PERFORMED BY THE DESIGNATED RIDER!

The smell of beef stew wafted in from the kitchen.

George closed the lid on the box and set the instructions aside for later.

⫿⫿ ⫿⫿⫿ ⫿⫿

George was three bites away from finishing his dinner when June caught him staring at the breezeway door for the second time. 'I'm sure it's not going to leave without you,' she said.

'What's that?'

'Your automatic bicycle.'

'Autonomous bicycle,' said George.

'Same difference.'

George finished his stew, got up and rinsed his bowl in the sink. 'I'll be in the garage,' he said. He wasn't about to wait for another snide remark from this wife. The breezeway door closed behind him without incident.

The sun had set but it was a warm summer evening. George turned on the garage lights. He immediately began removing parts from the shipping box. He saved the middle section, which was quite heavy, for last. Assembly was rather straight-forward – a wheel here, a wheel there, seat, handlebars – all put together using a special multifunction tool provided, although he still managed to break a fingernail in the process. The bicycle was equipped with a spring-loaded kickstand for parking ease. Once assembled, George stood back. The overhead fluorescents sparkled off the bicycle's metallic blue frame. The chrome accents added just the right touch of sophistication. Aesthetically, it was a work of art.

George returned to the instruction booklet. **SECTION 11: PROGRAMMING.** This section included several tree diagrams and many words in bold letters. He skimmed the introduction, mumbling to himself.

'Apply root hair, saliva or blood into the biometric receptacle...'

George lifted the front panel on top of the built-in motor. There was a small depression with the words SAMPLE printed above. He referred to the booklet.

'Blood is optimal...'

George hadn't thought this far ahead. He had read the literature but had somehow missed mention of bodily fluids. But then how else would the bicycle be in sync with its driver? Pedal exertion? Braking habits? If it wanted blood, then blood it would be!

George stared at his broken fingernail. He gripped the torn flap with thumb and forefinger and, taking a deep breath, quickly pulled. The pain was more than he had expected. He'd not only torn the nail but a thin strip of skin below the cuticle. A deep red welled from the furrow. 'That ought to do,' he said, squeezing the blood into the receptacle. He then pressed PROCESS and sucked on his finger while he waited.

The bicycle motor sputtered and coughed and after several false starts it hummed a pleasant tone like a soft continuous wind chime.

ENTER VOICE COMMAND

A COMMAND CAN BE AS SIMPLE AS ONE WORD

OR A PHRASE (I.E. *HELLO! LET'S GO!*

EASY PEASY LEMON SQUEEZY).

George thought for a moment. A smile graced his lips. He leaned into the microphone and said, 'Hi-ho Silver, away!'

The lights on the autonomous bicycle blinked and flickered.

PROCESSING COMPLETE

George then sat on the automated beauty for the first time. He turned the wheel left then right. He bounced on the seat like a child on holiday. The bicycle was now ready for its maiden voyage. There were three options on the control panel: **STREET MAP**, **OFF-ROAD** and **RANDOM**. George was about to make a selection when the breezeway door opened and June called out to him. 'Are you coming in?' She appeared annoyed that he was spending so much time with his new toy.

'Dear, you should see this. It's an amazing piece of engineering. I can't wait to take it out.'

'Tomorrow, George. There's always tomorrow.' June turned then and entered the house, presumably expecting George to follow. But George was feeling adventurous, impulsively autonomous in his own right. A short evening ride seemed like the right thing to do.

Before he changed his mind, he mounted the autonomous bicycle, pressed **RANDOM**, shouted 'Hi-ho Silver, away!' and, as advertised, away he went.

Without the luxury of anticipating the bicycle's movements, it was all George could do to keep from sliding off the seat at every turn. It wasn't until George realised that he could simply keep an eye on the illuminated travel screen and see the course ahead, albeit not too far in advance, but far enough to prepare for upcoming stops and turns.

He had made it to the end of his road in one piece and now turned onto the main thoroughfare that headed east toward the centre of town. One of the reasons George purchased the autonomous bicycle was that he believed the area in which he lived was ideal for touring. There were unclogged streets, bridges, a causeway, and being a coastal town there was a boardwalk that hugged the sea.

The bicycle took another turn. It seemed to be circling back home. Nothing adventurous this time, thought George, taking in the evening stars. He pretended to pedal even though it was unnecessary. He glanced into the residential windows he passed – miniature movie screens of people's lives: washing dishes, watching television, dressing up or dressing down for the evening.

The bicycle suddenly braked to avoid hitting a cat that had darted into its path. George nearly toppled over the handlebars. The cat ran off. George's heart continued to pump as the bicycle picked up speed again. Despite the near-miss it was a good feeling. George felt alive.

But George's excitement was short-lived, as June was waiting for him in her nightgown when the bicycle pulled into the driveway.

'Couldn't wait, could you? And you can wipe that grin off your face.'

George couldn't help it. He hadn't felt like this in a long time. The bicycle returned to its original spot in the centre of the garage. The kickstand lowered automatically and George got off the seat. The bicycle powered down.

George rushed over to June and picked her up and swung her around, all the while planting a big kiss on her lips. 'Thank you,' he said, setting her back down. She eyed him suspiciously. 'For what?' She tried to stay angry but George's excitement was infectious. She let a rare smile creep across her lips.

'For that,' George said, pointing to her face. 'I'm going to make some tea.' George had a skip in his step on his way into the house.

'Kettle's already on,' said June, still eyeing the autonomous bicycle. She was thinking crazy, dangerous thoughts – thoughts that sent an unexpected sliver of anticipation through her veins. At last, she shut the light off and joined her husband.

⊹⊹⊹

The following day George rose early. He was on his bicycle while the grass was still damp with dew. Again, he selected RANDOM and the bicycle took him along a lazy route that wound up through the countryside. George never realised how hilly the terrain was just five miles inland. One particular hillside rose up above the rest. The bicycle navigated a narrow lane with crumbling stonewalls on either side. An old farmhouse sat near the top. There was a **For Sale** sign driven into the ground at the edge of the yard. Sheep dotted a lush green pasture. At last, the bicycle rolled to a stop. George couldn't believe the view.

The entire coastal village lay below, a picture postcard of quaint homes, restaurants and boutiques, and beyond, the deep blue of the ocean as far as the eye could see. It was breath-taking. It was a world of possibilities. Was it purely coincidental or was the bicycle showing George this for a reason?

George's heart beat nervously in his chest. He'd always dreamed of owning a property such as this, ever since he was child. Except instead of sheep he envisioned horses. It was too coincidental to be coincidental, thought George.

At last, he selected a destination: home. At first, the bicycle refused to move. The bleating of sheep floated on the air, but in George's ears it sounded like the braying of a horse. George typed in his address using the keypad instead and the bicycle lurched forward toward the edge of the cliff before settling into reverse. Once turned around, it carried George home without incident.

⫼⫼ ⫼⫼⫼ ⫼⫼

Spooked by the autonomous bicycle's brazen autonomy, George didn't ride it for a week. It sat in the garage looking shiny and new and eager to take him to shiny and new places. It scared him and he didn't know why. He puttered around the house instead, fixing things he'd promised June he'd fix since he'd retired. June asked him only once why he wasn't out gallivanting with his newfound friend. He hugged her then and confessed that maybe he was getting too old for adventures. She smiled and said, 'Don't return it just yet.'

No *I told you so*. No victory lap. George believed June was being her usual contradictory self; it was one of the many reasons he loved her. When Saturday came he understood why she was so understanding. A truck arrived in the morning, the very same truck that had arrived two weeks earlier, only this one delivered June's very own autonomous bicycle.

'Why, you devil,' said George, both proud and a little bit unnerved by his wife's autonomous action.

'I figured why should you be having all the fun?' Her smug expression was as adorable as when they had first met.

'I love you,' he said.

She nodded. 'You better. Now, get lost while I put this together.'

George left her in the garage with her new baby.

That evening George and June took their respective bicycles and selected a street map location as their destination: an Irish pub that served corned beef sandwiches and red ale. The bicycles followed the exact same route, slicing through the warm air with a soothing hum. They ate out for the first time in ages, talked about things they hadn't discussed in years – not since the children had moved away. Things like dreams and ambitions and a life of possibilities – possibilities they assumed had passed them by, but now, with the autonomous bicycles, spurred thought and discussion and even spirited debate.

When it was time to head home it was June's turn to select RANDOM. 'Are you sure?' said George, a furrow of genuine concern on his brow.

'Why not?' said June. 'See you back at the ranch!' And off she went.

George couldn't very well follow her because if he were to select RANDOM he would be off in his own random direction. He could only watch her go, waving as she disappeared from sight. He programmed his own bicycle for home and once there waited for her.

The seconds stretched to minutes, the minutes to an hour. He waited longer than he probably should have. 'Dammit June!' he said angrily before shutting the television off and grabbing the car keys.

But when he got into the car he realised he didn't know where to go. Random was random. June could have gone anywhere. What if the autonomous bicycle had led her into a dangerous part of town? What if June's driving inexperience had caused her to plunge headlong into a ditch? What if she was stranded, incapacitated and in need of his help? He didn't know what else to do except wait for her call, if one indeed was forthcoming.

And then a thought occurred. He got out of the car and got onto his autonomous bicycle. He typed in a new destination on the keypad: JUNE.

The bicycle seemed to think for a moment. A strange vibration came from the processing unit and then, miraculously, a destination was found: a small dot on the sea coast several miles north of where they had eaten.

'Hi-ho Silver, away!' George said.

This time the autonomous bicycle chose a more direct route, bypassing the way he and June had gone to the pub. George zipped along suburban side streets and rural roads and eventually onto the coastal highway. The bicycle turned down one of the many private lanes and he was soon at the entrance to a public beach parking lot. The lot was closed for the evening but the bicycle slipped through the space between the chain post and a concrete barrier, and aimed straight for the footpath that led to the beach. He found June's bicycle parked in the sand. June sat on the beachhead, facing the ocean.

'June? What's going on?' George had left his bicycle beside hers and navigated the shifting sand to join her. June's face was wet with tears.

'I'm sorry,' she said, 'I was about to head home but I couldn't bring myself to leave just yet.'

'That's okay, I found you. Well, actually, my bicycle found you. I was just along for the ride.'

She laughed then. She looked over her shoulder at the two bicycles standing in the sand. One leaned one way while the other leaned the opposite. June's smile receded like the waves.

'I used to come here with my mother.'

'You never told me that,' said George.

'It was because my father was a bastard.'

'Oh.'

'When he drank, my mother would bring me here and we'd spend the day, putting off going home as long as possible.'

'I didn't know.'

'She could never relax. She was always looking over her shoulder.' As June spoke, the low-tide ocean waves provided a quiet backdrop like the slow breaths of a sleeping giant. 'Of course, I didn't know what was going on at the time. I was just a happy-go-lucky kid. But, looking back, this was the place where I always felt safe.' She turned to look at George. 'How did it know?' The emphasis on the word "*it*" implied she was talking about the bicycle.

George scrambled for an answer. 'Just like mine knew where to find you. Maybe it can read us in ways that we can't read ourselves?'

'By using our blood?'

'Well, no. I think it's more than that. I think it's in the way we assembled it, brought it into being. In a way, we give birth to it with our touch, our voice, and, yes, maybe our thoughts and our desires.'

'You think so?'

'Yup. And one other thing.'

'What's that?'

'I think it just wants us to be happy.'

For a moment, June stared at the ocean waves. Again, she turned to look at George. 'Are you happy, George?'

George could tell by the shakiness in her voice that June wasn't sure of the answer she'd hear, but she was willing to risk asking if it meant hearing the truth.

'Of course I am. Are you?'

June appeared to consider her answer. 'You know, I have to be honest, when *it* started taking me away from town, I didn't know what to think. I didn't know if I should hit the brakes or just let it take me. But the curious thing is a part of me wanted to go. I wanted to experience something different, even if it meant experiencing it without you. It was frightening. But it was also exciting.' She took George's hand. 'I'm sorry.' Moonlight glistened in her eyes.

'Don't be sorry.' George told her about his trip to the hilltop farm overlooking the bay. 'It would be a great place to spend our remaining years,' he said. 'A place to invite the grandchildren over to ride the horses.'

'Horses?'

'Yes, horses. I've always wanted horses. Not to ride. Just to watch them be... horses. I know that sounds silly.'

'No, it doesn't sound silly at all.'

'We have the savings. We could sell the house.'

June nodded. She could hear in his voice how much it meant to him. 'We should look into it.'

An uneasy silence followed.

'And to answer your question,' she said. 'I am happy, but...'

'Uh-oh.'

'Let's say we do get the farmhouse, we still need to get out more. Explore. Do the things we used to do when we first met.'

George kissed her, tasting happy tears. 'Deal,' he said.

They held onto each other as the ocean waves breathed a sigh of relief. But a thought occurred to George. He looked at June with concern. 'But how are we going to explore when *they* seem to want us to explore on our own?'

June thought about it. 'Well, I guess we'll just have to trust that they'll lead us back home. Wherever that may be,' she said.

᛫ᛁᛁᛁ᛫ ᛫ᛁᛁᛁᛁᛁ᛫ ᛫ᛁᛁᛁ᛫

The following morning, June's theory was put to the test. Both she and George prepared for their individual adventures, each with drinking water and snacks in their travel packs, for they didn't know how long they would be gone or even where they were going. They mounted their autonomous bicycles simultaneously and called out their starting commands. The bicycles came to life.

'Well?' said George, 'are you ready to do this?'

'Are you?' said June. She smiled nervously.

'Random?' said George.

June nodded her head. 'Random it is.'

Each entered the **RANDOM** command and off they went, down the driveway and onto the street. To their mutual surprise they shadowed each other for the first mile, then the next, and the five more that followed until they reached the farmhouse on the hill, where they got off their bicycles and knocked on the door. An elderly woman greeted them.

'Hi,' said June. 'My husband and I are very much interested in buying your farm. Would you mind if we take a look around?'

'Be my guest,' said the woman.

Afterward, when they were ready to get back onto their autonomous bicycles again, George looked at June and simply shook his head.

'What?' she said.

'After all these years, you still surprise me.' He leaned over and kissed her. 'I love you,' he said.

She looked at him – the man she'd married. He was still there in those eyes of his. The face might be older, but it was wiser and as handsome as ever. 'You better,' she said.

And off they rode, into the future, together.

Limbo

*Layla
Sakamoto
Sharifi*

Time stopped for Arya Ahmadi and their family that week, and for the second time in their relatively short life, they were forced to contend with the heaviness of the supernatural. The world kept going – the subway was still full of grinding commuters, the stores were still full of consuming shoppers, and the building's elevators kept moving up and down, full of people moving through time. But in the Ahmadis' cramped two bedroom apartment on the Upper West Side, behind the off-white door with the almost-broken-doorknob – time stopped. It started gradually, just like the first time. The Ahmadis hardly noticed it. The bathtub would fill up slower than normal, Arya's brother's basketball wouldn't bounce back up as fast, their usually speedy internet loaded pages at a pace reminiscent of the '90s. They attributed it to faulty pipes, a flat ball, a congested network. The mind rarely goes to the supernatural, usually trying to make sense of the senseless. But once the water stopped altogether, the ball refused to come back up, and the internet shut down, they had to take notice.

⑆ ⑈ ⑆

It began on a shivery Saturday morning. The mild winter had come to a head that week – snow freezing into fields of brown ice across the sidewalks, pedestrians having to slow their brisk paces to avoid catastrophe. Arya, 25, was sitting on their sage green bedspread (chosen for the calm the colour elicited) in their sanctuary of a room, watching the thin January sunlight fight its way through the low Crown Heights buildings, through their foggy window, and to the tips of their fingers. They were fully dressed in unwrinkled slacks and a matching vest – baggy to hide their slight frame – and thirty minutes early as always, preparing their body and nerves for the busy Soho café shift that was to come. Their dark hair was closely cropped for convenience and gender euphoria and their face was as bare as the room it lived in.

The phone rang.

Arya? Their mother whispered with a tone she had never uttered before. Panicked, out of breath, a departure from her usual upbeat strength. You should come here quick. Dad fell.

On the ride uptown, Arya couldn't keep up. The train glided swimmingly, New Yorkers gliding with it, avoiding the usual unexplained jerks and sudden stops, but Arya's muscles were stagnate with resistance and they couldn't turn their eyes to notice. All they could focus on was the single possibility slowly pulling through their mind – losing their father. Losing the glue that held their family together. Losing the rock that grounded them when they almost fell. Losing the guide that taught them how to be soft. They knew from a decade of therapy that speculating without facts would lead to unnecessary anxiety, but they couldn't remember any of their coping mechanisms. The subway creatures around them blurred, their fingers could hardly type for updates.

As they exited the station, Arya's parents' building loomed in front of them, its haughty French architecture seemingly mocking their fear. Ornate stone gargoyles turned to look as they passed – scorning at the lag surrounding their body, perhaps remembering the day Arya nearly put shame upon their precious home. Upper West Siders walking by glanced disdainfully at the tall sluggish rogue blocking their path. Arya noticed nothing. They were consumed with step step stepping each steel-clad toe upon the flowing pavement, push push pushing the fortified revolving door, walk walk walking into the hyper-speed elevator that stopped. At. Ten.

They dragged their feet along the wide carpet of the bright hallway that darkened around them as if the light could not reach their body. Halting before the off-white door with the almost broken doorknob as if something in their bones sensed wrongness, they opened the door and looked around – no one was home and everything was as if everyone could be back at any moment. The dishes still laid carefully stacked to prevent chipping in the deep kitchen sink, the bathroom door still closed shut to uphold feng shui, the fruit plate and teapot still sat on the low circular coffee table: the remnants of breakfast. No one would be home for hours – Arya's mother was gathering stoicism in the emergency room, Arya's brother was practising lay-ups in a church basement fifteen blocks away, Arya's father was trying to figure out what year it was. Unsure whether to feel unsettled or relieved at the normalcy around their immediate surroundings, Arya collapsed onto the grey tufted couch – falling as if in slow motion, falling as if time could not flow around their tired body.

Arya remembered this feeling, or at least their body did. Their mind refused to admit that it could be happening again. The first time, an era of dark magic loomed over them – ageing them beyond their years, bestowing trauma and stress upon their young fluid body, turning them solid from the inside out. That density ultimately let them break back into the flow of passing time with sheer force and power, but it cost them their softness. They promised to never let time stop again, to use their newfound strength to break it if necessary, but Arya was no match for time. So for now, they were in denial. They had enough to focus on elsewhere.

Arya's brother, 15, got home from basketball practice later that day. He moved through the marble lobby seamlessly, flowing in youth and large strides, gliding in tandem with time. His movements had just started to become fluid again after a significant growth spurt the spring before had instilled awkwardness in his bones. As he entered the elevator, he ran his hand through the mop of dark hair on his elegant head, glancing in the mirror to make sure his shirt was half tucked into the basketball shorts that sat perfectly low on his slim hips. He didn't notice that his parents weren't home, he didn't notice Arya's pitiful expression as he walked past them to his room, he didn't notice when Arya sat him down and told him what happened that his motions started slightly straggling. He didn't notice much these days outside of his friends, appearance, and three-point average.

Arya's mother, 58, came back from the hospital that night. A delay surrounded her usual swift pace as she walked home, as it had bound her muscles in the flying ambulance, as it had engulfed her brain in her corner of the ER. Her long coarse hair, dyed carefully black to cover the grey coming in, was uncharacteristically dishevelled; the designer jumpsuit that she threw on before boarding the ambulance was rumpled. She was totally fine though – her seemingly healthy husband had a seizure and couldn't remember her name, but she was totally fine. A little tired maybe, but totally fine, totally fine, totally fine!

Arya's father, 61, returned the next day with great fanfare. Something was wrong, and no one knew what it was, but getting out of the hospital void was a cause for celebration. Arya's mother cooked steak – rare for everyone but hers medium well – and Arya's brother, in rare form, spent the evening outside of his room. Arya's mother noticed that her steak took ten minutes longer than it usually would, but she decided it was due to the new brand of meat she had decided to try. Arya noticed their father seemed depressed – he rarely looked up, moved heavily, and got into bed as soon as dinner was over, but they chalked it up to a long day at the hospital. Arya always seemed to notice things about their father that their other family members didn't see. Arya's brother noticed nothing.

Tests would continue throughout the week, slowly slowly on hospital time. His preliminary X-rays showed shadows in the lungs, but no worries! That could mean anything! A mild infection, tuberculosis, canc–anything! No worries.

Arya decided to stay on their parents' couch for the time being.

⫼ ⫼ ⫼

On Monday morning, CAT scans came back with more shadows. The lightbulbs in the apartment dimmed. Arya tried replacing them, but the new ones didn't work.

On Tuesday morning, the Ahmadis woke up to a cold apartment. The radiators were barely emitting heat, which in the -3°C January winter meant bundling up under turtlenecks, sweaters, coats, fuzzy socks, blankets. Arya's father slept all day. Arya, unable to face him in his weakness, spent the day trying to keep busy. Having found that none of their phones had enough signal after trying to call the super, they left to knock on his door. He was too busy to come take a look but gave them a few space heaters for the time being. Those didn't seem to work either.

On Wednesday morning, the brain MRI came back with spots. The internet shut off.

On Thursday morning, Arya's brother tried to take a shower before school and found that the water wasn't running. Nonchalant as always, he showered at the gym at school. Arya's body knew what was happening, but their consciousness tried to call the super again. They didn't lose faith when their cell phone still didn't work in the apartment, picking up a dusty landline and listening for a tone. When they didn't find one, Arya dragged out their father's toolbox and started twisting at the shower's knobs as if they knew what they were doing.

On Friday morning, the hospital called. None of their phones worked, but they left a message and Arya was able to get a thin signal outside the building. There was to be an appointment with Dr. Pereyra on Monday morning to discuss bronchoscopy results and treatment. Arya went to the hospital to look her up, straining at the effort it took to walk ten blocks. She was the top thoracic oncologist in the city. The water, lights, and heat finally shut off.

ıllı· ·ıllllı· ·ıllı·

The weekend stretched into nothingness. The Ahmadis checked into a hotel across the street while the heat, water, lights, internet and phone were being sorted out. Maintenance could not figure out what went wrong. Everything seemed to work perfectly when they got there.

The Ahmadis faced more problems at The Ingraham Hotel. The lights kept flickering, the phones kept cutting out, and the water dribbled out of the spout. The room was unusually dark and the expected sirens and honks of Broadway outside the window were nowhere to be found.

Arya's brother spent the weekend with his many friends. He knew in the back of his mind that he should be with his father, but could not bear to be confined in the inadequate hotel room having to notice the deterioration of his family members. At his basketball game on Saturday, he started to notice that his muscles had slowed down. Arya, the only one who showed up, noticed that he, the shooting guard, didn't make any three-pointers. He couldn't muster up the time to shoot before being blocked – the other team won. After the game, alone in the locker room, Arya's brother threw his water bottle at the wall with all of his strength. He watched as it slowly left his hand, almost floating into the plaster. As it tapped the wall, it fell suddenly, clanging loudly onto the floor. Arya felt his frustration, but kept their distance, unsure of what to say or do. His friends noticed nothing.

Arya's mother spent the weekend reading her favourite Murakami novels. Usually a voracious reader, she only got through a third of one book. She attributed it to the stress of moving to a third-rate hotel, with crummy light, uncomfortable beds, and dead bugs everywhere. She complained to the front desk, but the new room they moved to was worse. She felt like she had aged twenty years that week – her bones creaked, her joints dawdled, her mind felt sedated, but she would never admit it. She kept telling herself that she was fine, fine, fine!

Arya's father slept for the whole weekend. He woke briefly to find his body would not work properly. He shut his eyes and went back to sleep.

Arya tried to show up to work on Saturday after getting their shifts covered all week, but they couldn't keep up with the morning rush and were sent home by their boss. They wandered around Washington Square Park for a little before heading to their brother's basketball game, but felt dizzy and nauseous from the rapid pace of the Saturday morning bustle.

Sunday felt like an eternity. Arya couldn't help being reminded of when time slowed down the first time, when their body couldn't get out of bed from the heaviness, when their mind told them none of it was worth it. When they were drowning inside of themself, reaching futilely for an escape from floods of sweltering hatred that reached every untouched crevice inside of their cavity of a body. When their numb brain would have difficulty grasping the slippery thoughts that occasionally slid around their skull, eventually giving up to watch the silvery beauties with envy. When time would ruthlessly rip apart their skin every night, leaving them pink and raw and bare. When the morning would give them back their skin and they would slip it on with effort – it was always tighter than the day before.

How strange that death refused them when they ached for it, but now haunted them when they forgot it.

When time stopped the first time, they tried to shield their family from their pain. They vowed years ago to never let time get the best of them again. This time, their body could feel itself slowing down further and further and its surroundings with it, but their mind told it to keep going. Go to the pharmacy to get their father's pain pills. Go to Sunrise Mart to get their mother nice shoyu. Go to various restaurants and cafés to drop off resumes after being fired from their job. Go to their building to check up on the progress of the apartment.

On Monday morning, Arya, their mother, and their father gingerly climbed into the back of a taxi to head to their appointment. They reached the hospital before any of them could finish putting on their seatbelts.

The tall sleek glass building towered over the three of them. Its standoffish exterior told them they were not welcome, that their lag had no place in its highly efficient interior. The elevator sped up to the seventeenth floor before any of them could process, and they were called into the doctor's office before any of them could sit down in the cold waiting room.

The Ahmadis trudged down the long hallway, tugging their bodies behind them. The bright fluorescent lights could not reach any of them, a cloud of darkness surrounding the group as they moved slowly slowly slowly. None of them noticed, each person focusing on their individual step step stepping towards their fate.

Dr. Pereyra strode into the room with gusto. Her white coat billowed behind her as if it couldn't keep up with her swift pace. The Ahmadis could not keep up either. They could hardly see her or hear her despite her proximity and as she talked rapidly, her voice seemed to run further and further away. As she spoke, then paused, one phrase jumped out at them and halted in front of their faces, blacking out the sterile room around them.

Stage four lung cancer.

The phrase envelops their ears and eyes and lips and noses and bodies, depriving their senses until they are each alone – without body, without breathing, without being. The room disappears, Dr. Pereyra disappears, and the Ahmadis split – each transported to their own unknown.

Time stops.

ılı· ·ıllıı· ·ılı·

Arya is back.

Back to the seventeenth floor roof, back to the day years ago when everything almost became nothing. They are standing on a grey platform that juts out from the embellished stone, facing the expansive city that raised them. The bitter January wind rushes through their long black hair and baggy clothes, but they don't seem to feel the cold. Their bones grind as their legs slowly take them further and further towards the edge. The stone gargoyles turn away in shame as their knees heavily bend. They see their family in their mind, yelling, reaching towards them, but Arya knows they won't get to them in time.

Time has pried them open, leaving their insides exposed and tender, defenceless against the cruelties of life, vulnerable to the promises of death.

Arya jumps with flourish, arcing through the air with the grace that sixteen years of ballet taught them, rising, then falling falling falling twirling slowly like a leaf from a tree, glass and stone and metal floating past them, the ground rising closer and closer. They close their eyes, readying themself for the hit, but it never comes – darkness and silence softly and comprehensively enveloping their body instead.

The building disappears, the ground disappears, and Arya is transported outwards. Time stops.

ı|ı· ·ı|||ı· ·ı|ı·

Arya thinks they might have died. They cannot see or hear or feel: in fact, their body seems to be missing. They can't quite remember what that body looks like, what the person attached

135

to that body feels like. Now that they think about it, they aren't quite sure if they are a person at all. Are they a whale? An amoeba? A universe?

As they adjust to a state of unbeing, they notice they can sense things, not with their eyes or ears or nose or tongue, but with their awareness of space. Actually, they can sense the entirety of time stretched out in front of them as they float outside of it.

They are in the apartment behind the off-white door with the broken doorknob, but they are also on the windy roof, also in the harsh hospital room, also nowhere at all. They are falling onto a couch, jumping off of a building, reeling in a metal chair. They are holding a stillborn baby to their heavy bosom, they are watching their comrades drop like missiles around their muscled legs, they are picking up shrivelled tomatoes from the dry unforgiving ground, they are propelling their tail fin through the water as they vocalise to their pod, they are extending fingers of protoplasm towards dead animal matter, they are stretching, expanding, letting dark energy push their galaxies apart, searching, hungry for more more more.

Sometimes they stay on the outside of time, never existing, never re-entering. Sometimes they re-enter, but with mind split from body, softness split from strength, fragmented. And sometimes, suddenly, they are Arya, with the cropped hair and the baggy jeans, with the tense shoulders and the anxious eyes, with their mind in their body, with their softness in their strength, behind the off-white door with the broken doorknob.

⑊⑊⑊

Arya's brother comes back to the hotel after school and is surprised to find that the room is empty. He is so surprised that he doesn't notice that his phone is working in the room again. He tries calling his father, then his mother, then Arya, but no one answers. He sits on the cold grey bedspread, bouncing a bit as the mattress gives under his weight, focusing his gaze on a brown spot on the ugly floral wallpaper. He hangs his perfectly coiffed head in his growing hands and weeps.

⫼ ⫼ ⫼

Arya's father comes to in his bed, in his apartment on the Upper West Side. He doesn't remember how he got from the hospital to his bed, what happened in that undetermined period of time or untime, but he doesn't seem to mind. The setting sun is creating patterns on the cream walls, and his wife is sleeping peacefully beside him. His long, slim body still feels heavy and slow, but he is able to lift his limbs to get out of bed. The room is cold, and as he lowers his hand near the radiator, he feels no warmth. He sighs knowingly, remembering how long it took for Arya to come back to time the first time. How his wife had held him as he wept for his child's pain. They haven't held each other like that in years. He picks up his phone, sees that there is one bar of service and a missed call, and calls his son.

⫼ ⫼ ⫼

Later that morning, the Ahmadis move their things back into their apartment – maintenance could find nothing wrong with the heating, water, internet, lights or phone. As soon as they move back, everything starts malfunctioning again, but the Ahmadis don't seem to care. The four of them are sitting around the brown and black coffee table, each on an individual lily pad cushion. The room is cold in temperature, but warm in ambiance – with handmade cards and drawings littering the walls, colourful blankets and pillows thrown about the grey tufted couch, and the remnants of breakfast sitting forgotten on the table. Arya, in a sage green pyjama set and unwashed hair, sits to the left of their mother, whose wrinkled nightgown flows around her body, who sits to the left of Arya's father, whose thinning curly black hair and prominent nose brim with life. He sits to the left of Arya's brother, in an untucked shirt and ruffled hair, who is noticing things, maybe for the first time.

His family, dangling on a precipice, infiltrated by a fracture. His father might die, his father who always played ball with him on family trips, who took off work to take him across the country, who taught him how to be simultaneously masculine and soft, who taught him how to love with all of his might. His father, who is facing his own death, is finding a death already growing inside him. His mother, whose overbearing positivity blinded her from acceptance, is decaying from a lack of touch, of connection, of tenderness. His sibling, whose strength saved their life and killed their softness, is losing bits of themself to hold their family together. And him, his faux ambivalence protecting the depth of his uneasiness, he is frozen in fear.

No lights are on, but the thin sunlight shines through the window, illuminating a tear on Arya's brother's cheek as he faces his family.

So there's treatment for the lung cancer? he whispers.

Yes, there is. Isn't that wonderful? Arya's smiling mother is optimistic as always. It won't cure it – it can't be cured, but if it works it will prolong it, Arya firmly adds. Ok. Arya's brother readjusts his legs. Will dad die?

Arya's mother's smile falters. Arya's parents look at each other, waiting for the other to respond. Neither of them want to tell their baby that his father might not make it to his high school graduation.

We all die eventually, Arya's father finally says, holding his hand out to his son. So yes. But this treatment will hopefully give us some time.

And what do we do when time runs out? Tears are shining on Arya's brother's cheek. Arya crawls over to their little brother and holds him in their arms, just as they did when he was a baby. They don't know the answer. None of them have thought that deeply, that honestly.

After a moment, Arya's father speaks up.

We will prepare ourselves for it. We will hold our connections to one another. We will love each other visibly and fiercely. And when I'm gone, you will make sure that you hold onto each other stronger than you ever have before.

Arya feels a hot tear slip down their cheek, then another, then another, flowing quickly and freely. Facing their father and letting him wrap an arm around their shoulder, Arya breaks down for the first time in years, body and mind in tandem with one another.

Arya's brother holds on to his older sibling as Arya's mother takes her husband's hand, her smile melting into the beginnings of acceptance.

Softness seeps into the Ahmadis' bones and they feel their muscles loosen, their lag lift. The lights turn on, the radiator starts emitting heat again.

Time starts.

Transition Island

*Olivier
Faivre*

The crabs came a few months later.

Our hair was already long and faded by the salt and the sun. Our beards had already grown grubby. But the island still felt new. We had gone around it once, before settling by the river. We had walked along the shore on the flaxen-clothed beach for three days and three nights and had noticed no difference between west, north, east and south. In every direction the ocean was limitless and the sky infinite. Back at the mouth of the river, we had set up camp under the shade of languid palm trees. We lived at the edge of a small estuary protected by a shoal of hypnotic-white sand. Behind us, the dense jungle fashioned a variegated tapestry of leaves, flowers and fruits. Before us, the young river lithely lost itself into the ocean. The air was heavy with sweet tropical scents and brimmed with the droning and stridulating of insect life. We lived naked, carefree, tranquil. The river provided water; we drank from the fresh cold stream. The ocean provided food; we scoured the tide pools for grooved clams, conical limpets, oval abalones. We lived simply, humbly, peacefully – that much we had learnt from our previous world – we lived a full, contented life every day; then a new one. One night, a starry vault indistinguishable from all the previous starry vaults, from the sea came the crabs.

The night was still and cold like trauma.

Clack!

We heard the frantic scurry of a thousand jointed legs.

Chirp!

A mechanical rubbing and gnawing covered the distant hum of the ocean.

Clap!

A thousand clawed feet clambered up our legs, then our abdomens, then our faces.

Screech!

A thousand serrated mandibles nibbled at hair, tunics, food scraps. A chemical odour – iodine, salt, ammonia – covered our warm musky animal scent. In the moonlight, a swarm of black marbles shined, some small as a nail, some large as a newborn. The beach was covered by an inchoate moving shadow, an oil spill of dark fractal tentacles.

Suddenly they were gone; our senses felt blunted; the crabs had occupied us wholly; they left a formless emptiness behind. Belatedly, slowly, gloriously, the sun rose, orange sunbeams carving the morning clouds into an exquisite peach organdie cloth. We found one of us lying motionless, rigid, eyes open. We could not tell whether the crabs entered first by the mouth or by the anus; the relentless work of a thousand razor-sharp mandibles had grotesquely disfigured both orifices. When we lifted the mutilated body, we felt it was empty; it had been carved and eaten from inside. We buried it in a simple mound at the top of the beach, a tumulus built in the sand like how children build a castle.

The crabs came back every night.

Every morning, we disposed of another empty, defaced shell in the tumulus. At first we felt an old urge to flee, to fight, to grieve. But the rhythm of the island felt as natural as ebb and flow; its regularity had the force of a constant. And our minds were strong; we had learnt to marvel and embrace and celebrate. We felt a great elation then; our senses became keener; our hearts became purer. Every feeling, every thought, moved our whole being. We drank water and it was deliciously fresh. We ate a nut, a shellfish, a blade of seaweed and felt the greatest rapture. We looked at the world in wonder, body and soul dancing in unison, and life was perfect like a circle. The tumulus grew into a small dune.

Soon we were all dead.

Then the crabs stopped coming. Small, industrious sand bugs dispersed the remains of our camp. The tumulus collapsed into the ocean, lapped away by the waves and the tides. The wind erased our footsteps. The empty sky swallowed the echoes of our voices and the fierce sun glared out all traces of thoughts. The river transported our emotions like sediments and discharged them into the sea and flowed chirpily. The estuary was alive again; cockles, oysters, cuttlefish, shrimps, molluscs and crustaceans of all shapes clambered and scrambled onto the rocks. The beach woke up. The sand moved and whistled. The fronds of the palm trees rustled in the wind; the great vines rang and banged. Insects hissed and buzzed behind the heavy fluted curtains of the jungle. In every direction the waves crashed, the surf roared, the ocean growled. The island was anew wild and maiden.

Until the next group arrived.

The Trees

*N. G.
Bowie-Johnson*

Thick and fleshy and leafless, the Tree is so tall it scrapes the colour from the sky. This one is big, maybe the biggest Sten's ever seen, and will take at least two days to round. He can feel the ground change as they approach the Tree, can hear it too, the slippery scrape of the People's sled, replaced by a grinding, crunching slide – the compacted crust of the earth broken here by their waiting god.

Sten reaches for the handle of his bark trowel. Checks his deep blade and his shallow. Arrival should be a time of celebration, each Tree met with song. This time the People are quiet. They have arrived, but there is no next Tree.

One voice breaks out of the gathered silence, Hod singing out his thanks. Kel and their two children asleep in the sled. His song reminds Sten there is still time for the next Tree, they will not reach this one until morning.

He turns to join Hod's singing, but the music sticks in his throat. Nu is weaving her way toward him. They haven't spoken in fifty Trees, but she has not changed. Her legs are still strong, jaw stronger, hair alive in the sunlight, and her eyes suggest a different life. She strides up to his sled and rattles the sleeping tent.

'Uzu. Get out. Go to Lyssa.' The shade cloth draws back and Uzu's round face peers through, eyes drawn thin against waking. 'Out.' Nu grabs Uzu's arm and hauls him from the sled.

'What are you doing, Nu?' Sten finds his voice. 'Uzu, get back in there.'

Uzu, clutching at his roll of clothes, looks at Sten. Then at Nu. Shakes his head and stumbles away.

'I'm tired,' says Nu. 'We'll talk later.' She gives Sten a long look before pulling back the curtain and crawling into the shade.

They were friends, Sten and Nu and her sister Nissi. More than friends. Sten remembers hide-and-seek between the sleds, peeling bark worms from the supplies, and listening to elders' stories at the back. When they were old enough, they became hunters, trapping game in the lower branches of the Trees. Everyone said they would share a sled.

'I want to come,' said Nissi, every Tree. Tall for her age with the same stubborn jaw as Nu.

'No,' said Nu, every Tree, until they came to a Tree smaller than the rest, its branches closer to the earth, and said yes.

Nissi falls before they reach the first branch. She takes an age to hit the ground. Stubborn jaw locked tight. Not making a sound. Lips white, eyes wide.

Sten isn't sure if he truly remembers her expression, if it's possible he saw it in that moment, or if it's a nightmare born to haunt him. He does remember the way the ground blossoms, a web of cracks reaching delicately out from her body, the way red bubbles from her lips and her fingers scrabble in the dust.

Sliding down, Sten thought Nissi was looking at him, that she wanted to get up. But Nu held him back. She was already gone.

'It's time.' Nu's voice jerks Sten from his reverie, her breath warm on his neck. She touches his arm. 'Do you think it's out there?'

'What?'

'The next Tree.'

'There is always the next Tree.'

Twilight has grown dense over the caravan, and Sten feels the People around him leaning in, ears hungry, walking their work or resting in sleds. Uncertainty loud in their laboured breath, fear in their stuttering step.

'There is always the next Tree,' he repeats, louder this time. 'In the morning, we will see.'

Walk the path. Tree to Tree. Never stop. Never turn back. What if there is no next Tree? The idea is like blasphemy. It eats at the heart of all Sten believes.

'Why are you here?' he asks.

'To flee the worm. To follow the path.' Nu's smile mocks him. 'Why are you here?'

'You know what I mean.'

'You should sleep,' says Nu.

Above them the sky rumbles, wind gusting, grit snapping at his face. 'There will be a storm,' he says.

'Help me when it breaks. Sleep now.'

Holding the harness tight, Sten keeps walking. Nu, daughter of En and Peri. Her eyes sharp, tongue sharper, like the bite of the glass adder. He glances at her. She sees and turns her head fully towards him, dense curls frothing around her face. Her eyes and lips dyed black by the night.

'Will you walk the whole night?' she says. 'There is no one else to walk for you.'

'Uzu would have.'

Nu laughs, throaty, indulgent, as though he's a child.

Sten quickens his pace, belly burning. 'Why are you here? We haven't–'

'Since Nissi rested. Yes. Fifty Trees ago. Can we be friends?'

'Why now?'

'Is there ever a better time than now? Something is changing. There is no next Tree.'

Sten stretches his mouth and massages his jaw with a hand. 'You are right,' he says, shrugging out of the harness. Nu is nearly as tall as he, but her shoulders are narrow, and the straps need to sit higher on her chest. 'Wake me when the storm comes.'

Nu nods, watches until his feet are off the ground, then, grunting softly with the effort, keeps walking toward the Tree.

⫟⫟⫟ ⫟⫟⫟⫟ ⫟⫟⫟

When he wakes up, Sten can't see his hand in front of his face. The tent smells like blood and burnt air and he floats, confused, in the dark.

'Get up, stone man.' The wind whistles and dust patters against the tent. 'You can help me now.'

Sten checks the straps binding tent to sled, and the fastenings on the water pods behind – their bark bowed and faintly clammy. Outside, dust covers watchful moon and earth and still the Tree dominates their vision. Its soaring bulk a deeper darkness blotting out half the sky, branches moaning and shivering a thousand lengths above the ground.

Sten reaches out to take the harness and Nu hands him one loop but keeps the other. Together they drag the sled towards the others, clustering beneath the heaving sky, seeking protection from the wind. Beneath the Trees is best, safeguarded from the worst of the storm by its branches. The first flash of lightning washes over them, arcing across the sky. Sten is rested, the fizzing energy of the storm racing in his veins. In one breath he and Nu work against the dark, in the next the world disappears in light. The strike a thousand jagged branches reaching out of sky, tip to tip to kiss the branches of the Tree. Earth and sky bound for a moment. Then darkness rushes over the sleds along with the roar of light's passing.

Close to the others now, Nu hands him her strap and secures the sled to Hod's. He and Kel are working at their harness and smile when they see Nu. They catch the sled in front and Sten pulls the straps from his shoulders. Nu helps him, taking the right as he takes the left, looping them tight to the next sled's anchor. Her hands are nimble, tying off the knot and checking its tension. She holds a finger in the air, then dashes forward, skipping over jerking ropes. Sten falls back to help old

Pula, whose shaking hands keep missing the anchor. The wind is too loud for speech, but she nods when he gestures for her to sit down. There will be strength aplenty at the front, she does not need to spend herself. Sten holds her hand as she settles into her tent, then moves back towards the front.

Above them, the Tree calls the storm's fury to itself. The lightning leaps from the clouds into the Tree's arms, burrowing into its flesh, and with each strike the Tree shudders – but the storm is only a moment, the Trees are forever.

Sten joins the others weaving through the sea of sleds, vaulting, leaping, moving forward to help pull, checking tents are secure and ropes taut. He nearly misses Nu as they pass on either side of a sled. She turns mid jump to intercept him. Reaches for his arm. Her eyes wide, whites luminous in the flashing light, their brown heart dark.

She pulls Sten back towards his sled. Leans close to say something that's lost to the wind. He points at the snaking lines of People at the front. Hundreds of the People at work, bent almost parallel to the ground, faces shielded from the wind and dust.

Nu blinks and swallows but doesn't let go of his arm. A trickle of blood runs from a scratch above her eyebrow. Her eyelashes flicker, long and heavy. The world is a blur of noise and dust except for Nu. She leans in and kisses Sten. Lips warm against his own. He shudders, breath coming fast, the crack and rumble of the sky muted above him.

So close to his ear, this time her words are clear. 'There are many at the front. Come.' She pulls away and smiles at him, but her eyes are tired. 'It will be–' the rest of what she says is taken by the wind.

In the sled, Nu's hair is thick and soft and runs like water over the bed; it's black and long and smells like sugar syrup and incense.

⫻ ⫻ ⫻

The cloth of the roof glows red in the morning, as Sten listens to the rhythmic chop of blades against the Tree. Nu breaths evenly beside him, hands cupped beneath her cheek. The sleds will remain attached as they circle the Tree, and they could lie like this all day. Someone coughs outside.

'Sten.' The voice dry, hoarse from an old injury.

The flap is drawn aside before Sten can answer. He blinks against the glare, Peri's bulk outlined by the piercing bright. Muscle and bone stretched wide. A powerful man. Little Tree, the People call him. The light picks out the hollows and protrusions of a scar beneath his chin, highlights his clenching jaw. There is no warmth in Nu's father's eyes.

'Peri,' says Sten. He glances at Nu, at the bare skin of her shoulder and back, and Peri scowls.

'Get up,' says Peri.

Nu stirs, eyelids lifting lazily. She props herself up on one arm to look at Peri. 'Father.'

Peri's scowl becomes a grimace, then a line. 'Sita...'

Sten misses Nu's response, the sound of her childhood name a gushing rush of faded memory: of him and Nu and Nissi dancing at the head of the caravan, singing the walking songs, imagining fanciful worlds of green and blue. Then Nissi's hair is a halo, but she has forgotten how to breathe, and Peri is forbidding him and Nu to be together.

151

Sten pulls himself up and away from the memory. 'What is it, Peri?'

'Your father...' Peri looks at Nu. Frowns. 'He is still.'

Still. The word slows to a crawl, a sprawling mess of sound that Sten can't piece together. He is aware of Nu's hand on his shoulder, of Peri shaking his head, of the twist in his stomach and the gurgling heat of bile in his throat.

'What?'

'Your father is still. The *Metan* needs you. You will take your father's place until another is chosen.'

'He must be checking on someone...' says Sten. Not still. Madmen at the fringe are still. Not his father. His father is Guide.

'I was with him when he stopped,' says Peri. 'He is still. Gone from us. No longer of the People.'

'Let him be, father.' Nu's voice cracks. 'He knows what still means.'

Peri shakes his head, black hair a mane behind him. 'You are Guide now. This is a difficult time. Much needs to be discussed. There is no next Tree.'

'There is always the next Tree.' The words come unbidden, reflexive. 'Where is he?'

'Far behind us now. He stopped walking in the night.'

'Why did no one stop him?'

'You know we cannot.'

'Why didn't you stop him?'

'I tried.' Peri's voice is a growl. 'This is his choice. The still do not return.'

'Father-' Nu pleads. But Sten is already on his feet. This is his duty.

'I will come.'

Sten stumbles as he steps from the tent. His feet and arms seem to exist a great distance from his body, knees and elbows crude joints to manipulate them. Peri grabs his shoulder and steadies him. His limbs retract, and he is Sten again. Contained. Around them the People live their lives and carry out their work.

'We would not ask it of you, except that we must make the decision now.'

'Have you told the People my father is gone?'

'No,' says Peri. 'Eli, Fes, Midi, Sera, Enar, Hajek. Each of them wish to push on.'

'As it is said,' Sten says. 'Why haven't you told them?'

'As it is said.' Peri's brow furrows at the affirmation. 'We lose more each day, not just the elderly. Rest. Still. It is the same. Our People are failing and there is no Tree. We did not want to break them with news of your father.'

'You and the others. What do you want?'

'We want to turn back, return to the last Tree. To lose ourselves in the desert is a terrible end.'

Sten remains silent. He's heard the arguments, has left such things to those older and wiser. Now he is asked to decide.

The People form three lines at the front, at least ninety of his brothers and sisters working hard on the ropes, sweat glistening, breath heavy with need. They pull the greater load so others might harvest as much of the Tree's gift as possible.

Those who seek the hard bark run ahead: the first scoring the guideline, the second driving their blade deep, the third and fourth deeper still until the sheet of bark is free and they can tear it from the Tree. Next come those working the soft bark, and behind them those gathering flesh. The smell of sap is thick in his nostrils and water steams where it falls to the ground. He imagines the cold bark beneath his hand, the resistance of Tree flesh between his fingers. The Tree provides. Eat of its flesh, drink of its water. As it is said.

'Your father is the deciding vote. Six for, six against. Vote for life, your life, your People's lives. Let us live to argue the right of it.'

'What did my father think?'

'He would have gone on.' Peri stiffens beside him. 'And yet he is still. You will vote to turn back. It is right.'

'It is right…' repeats Sten. He watches as hunters leap onto the Tree and scramble up its trunk, bone shoes and picks biting deep. Within minutes they are shadows above him, hunting the birds and rodents in the lower branches. A welcome change from the soft bark that does not rot. They will eat well tonight.

'Good,' says Peri, assuming something that was never said.

⫶⫶⫶ ⫶⫶⫶⫶ ⫶⫶⫶

The *Metan* meets beyond the first sleds, friends he has known all his life, who loved his father and shared that love with his son. Now they are strangers, dressed in their ritual masks, white bark hiding their expression – hiding their skin and their soul. Only their eyes move.

'Your mask.' Peri holds it out to him. Inside it is leather and smells of blood and dust and family.

'Well met, Guide,' the nearest mask inclines its head towards him, voice made hollow by the bark.

Sten's mask is different. It is the Guide, the charcoal symbol on its forehead turned toward the next Tree. At least it should be.

The *Metan* talks of daily matters: of disputes between sleds and families; the distribution of load; the punishment for crimes. Over it all hangs the shade of his father and empty shadow of the next Tree.

In the mask you are no one. You are all who have come before, all the People who have worn the mask. Yet Sten is not those People, he is not his father, and he knows his voice is not his father's voice.

The sun traces its path across the sky and still the masks talk. They do not drink or eat, they only walk. Sten grows dizzy, cheeks burning against the leather, face melting into wood. He looks up at the sun, a lake of fire to consume the world.

One of the masks grunts and cuts their hand through the air impatiently. 'Enough. Let us vote. We must prepare the People to turn back. The longer we delay the more we risk fracture.'

Another mask turns to the first. '*The worm's flesh is poison, and its mouths are many.* You would damn us all.'

'No. In your blindness, it is you who damns us. *The path is set, walk the Trees and rest in their shade.* I see no Tree, no path, but that which lies behind us.'

'*All who would live, walk forward. Onward, the Trees.*'

'Over and over, we tread the same ground.' The voice is Peri's. 'Let the Guide speak.'

Twelve blank ovals turn towards Sten. The black of their eye and mouth holes swallows his thoughts. They are hungry for themselves. They worry for themselves. They are no more than the People they lead – who whisper unease, who look to the horizon and feel fear.

'The Tree will take a day to round.' He can't breathe, can barely speak for the dust in his mouth. 'I must think. Can we vote in the morning?'

'Vote now, boy. Let those of us with experience think. We must turn back.'

'You overstep yourself,' says another. 'He is Guide. If you need a night, boy, you shall have it. Know only that the longer we wait, the more the People waiver. We must walk somewhere.'

The other masks nod their agreement. The People must walk somewhere.

╷╷╷· ╷╷╷╷╷· ╷╷╷·

The sun is low on the horizon and soon Sten will walk and think. Nu is still there when he returns to his sled to gather his harness. 'I thought you'd be gone.'

She raises her chin and glares at him. 'Do you want me to go?'

'I don't know.'

Her eyes flicker.

'No.'

She smiles. 'Good.'

'I will walk tonight.'

'Then we have time.'

'Is this how I honour my father?' says Sten, lying tired on the sheets.

Nu touches his shoulder. 'Is it such a bad way?'

'Peri does not approve.'

'My father doesn't approve of anything.'

'He forbids it.'

'Will you always do only what our fathers say? You promised we would walk together.'

'Before Nissi...'

'Yes. Before Nissi died. Why didn't you come to me then? You should have come to me.'

Sten isn't sure what to say. 'I think–'

Nu waits for him.

'When I heard her fall, I looked, and I thought it was you. Part of me is still on that Tree, looking down at you.' He searches for something, but all he can think of are Nissi's eyes staring up at the sun. 'You remember, her eyes were open...'

'I remember.'

'I am a coward.'

'Yes.' Nu leans over and looks him in the eyes. 'You should have come.'

'Yes.'

'At least you know it.'

Soon Sten will walk to the front, lose himself in the work. It's what he is good at, he was never meant to be Guide. 'I have to decide.'

'To decide what?'

'To go on or go back. To choose between the desert, or the worm.'

Nu lies back, looking at the cloth of the roof and tracing the line of the sheet with her hand. 'Do you ever think of staying at the Tree?'

'No. Do you?'

She shrugs. 'I'm glad you don't. The People should keep walking.' She rolls to look at him. There are tears in her eyes. 'You are not yourself. You are Guide. You should do what is right for the People.'

'You are right. Night is coming. I should go.'

Nu nods and rises with him. Together they dress and make their way to the front. The other night walkers wind silent through the sleds, ready to give their brothers and sisters rest. Sten holds the rope in his hands, loops it over the bark guards on his chest and shoulder. It draws tight and he can feel the many hands that hold it. The People walk the Trees together, they trust each other to walk with them.

As the sun rises behind them, someone touches Sten's shoulder. He turns, thinking it is Nu. Instead, Dedeb smiles and indicates he hand her the rope. Nu is gone and already someone labours in her place. He gives up the rope and walks to the *Metan*. He puts on his father's mask – his mask – then looks out at the desert and waits for the others to arrive.

'*This alone is trustworthy*,' he begins, '*walk the Trees, despise the worm.* I am uncertain, but if we are to lead the People to their death, we should do it in the right. According to how we have lived. According to what we have believed. I say we go on.'

Some of the masks clasp hands and chant in unison. 'Onward, the Trees.' Sten can't bring himself to join them.

Several others turn without speaking and walk back towards the caravan. Peri tears off his mask, and crushes it beneath his foot, the crack echoing in the morning quiet. The sound of the mask's breaking rings in Sten's ears, as he walks back to the caravan with the others, unsure what he has done.

'At least your father had the good sense not to damn us all with his blindness.' Peri bears down on Sten from behind. Not so little, the Little Tree. His fists tight at his sides.

'I am not my father.'

'No. At least your father killed only himself.' Peri closes on him, raising an arm over his head. The blow breaks over Sten's back like a boulder. Knocks him to his knees. His hands scrape on the ground and his vision grows dark. He can't breath.

'Our People–' Peri's voice is muffled, as though he is whispering. 'Nissi–'

Sten looks up, sees People drawing close. Their mouths are moving, but he can't hear them. He watches the big man raise his arms again, hands clasped together, muscles bunched as he brings them down. A mountain falling towards Sten's head, enough to bury him. He thinks about letting it happen, at the last moment pulls back. Just enough. Air rigid as Peri's fists rushes past. He doesn't want to fight. Peri is right.

'Stop. Please.' Sten narrowly avoids another blow but doesn't see the next and it sends him sprawling, dust in his mouth and nose, grit grating against his teeth. It tastes like blood and death.

'Maybe father left, maybe–' he's not sure what he is saying, feels consciousness slipping, black edging his vision. Another image skates across his flagging mind. Peri standing like this, in the night, over the body of his father. Sten's scrabbling hands dislodge a knife-sharp blade of earth. 'Did you kill him?'

On Peri's face, confusion wars with frustration. 'What are you talking about?'

Sten sees in Peri's eyes that the imagined crime did not happen, even as Peri raises his fists again. But the image boils in Sten's mind, and he brings the blade-sharp earth up towards the other man's face, an inferno of rage and blame and guilt begging for release. At the last moment he drops it.

Peri's eyes go wide at what Sten was ready to do. The big man's hair is a halo around him. For a moment Peri's fists block out the sun, like a shade cloth snapped shut. Sten is swallowed by that shadow. Hands grab at him and pull him up and away. Voices swell around him. Nu is there, standing in a beam of sunlight. He sees her, watching him, her eyes empty. All he wants is to see them shine, to see them full to the brim with life.

'I'm sorry,' he shouts groggily. But the world is fading, and his words disappear into the dark. His only thought: that this is no way to be.

⫶⫶⫶ ⫶⫶⫶⫶ ⫶⫶⫶

Sten wakes with a start in the late afternoon. Head pounding, face brittle, the sun red and angry on the horizon. He needs to speak with Nu, to explain what happened. He aches to think she might reject him. Eyes burning, he steps from his sled and looks around. The gatherers are returned from the Tree, and are working to process the harvest: water squeezed from flesh, fibres hung, hard bark stacked, soft spread to dry. Their food for the journey.

'Where's Nu?' he asks, stumbling towards her family's sled.

People shake their heads. Avert their eyes. Eventually someone points back and Sten follows the arc of their arm, stumbling over ropes and bumping into sleds. But Nu is nowhere Sten can see.

In the distance, falling behind the caravan are scattered People. Some trudging slowly, as if to follow, others sitting or leaning against the Tree, a few lying stiff, fallen face down with no one to lift them. And there, helping one of the fallen sit against the Tree, is Nu. Sten runs to her, breaking from the People, not caring about the transgression.

She stands when she sees him, eyebrows raised. Shakes her head, mocking, as though he is a child. 'Go back, stone man.'

'Why?'

'Because you belong with the People.'

'I can't–' his throat is tight, as though he's swallowed dirt. 'You can't–'

'Sten.' She reaches up and touches his face, fingers tracing his eyebrow. 'You didn't make Nissi climb the Tree. You can't make me come with you.' She turns away and looks at the desert behind them. 'There is no worm. I'm sure of it. You know, I felt nothing when you and my father fought. Even when you could have killed him. You say a part of you died, when Nissi fell. I've died every day since then, until there is nothing left of me. I wondered what I'd feel if one of you died, and it is nothing. I am not of the People.'

'You can be. We could be. Together–'

'No.' She steps away from him. 'It was nice, stone man. It would have been nice, were we more than ourselves.'

'I–'

'Do you ever wonder? Where are we going? Do the Trees go on forever? Do we travel in a circle? Do we always turn back? Is this all there is? Is it right?' She gestures at the People sitting and fallen. 'They eat at me, the questions. If it does exist, I would meet the worm – walk the passage of its throat. Do you understand?'

'No.'

'Try. Try for me, and for my family. Be good for our People.' She leans in and kisses him, then, pulling away, she waves for him to leave. 'Go.'

'I could stay–'

She turns away from him to help the next of the fallen. She does not look back. 'Go.'

Sten watches her help each person in turn, moving further and further away, until he can no longer see her in the dark. Then he turns and follows the caravan.

Blind in the dark he walks for hours. The silence of the desert suffocating him, seeping into his mouth and nose, clogging his ears and pressing on his eyeballs. There is nothing. He is nothing. He is alone in the world and all it promises is the dark. It is a long time before he hears the sobbing, longer still before he realises it's his own. Even this has passed by the time he hears the grinding passage of the sleds. The People whisper as he walks past, cast furtive glances as he makes his way to Peri's sled. En steps out from the sled and raises a hand to stop him. 'En...'

She does not cry out, and no tear falls from her eye, but her face ages at the news.

'I should tell Peri,' says Sten.

'No,' says En. 'You shouldn't.'

That night, Sten's sled is empty, and Nu's questions echo through the dark.

⁂

The People walk onwards. The Tree behind them is swallowed by the earth and still there is no next Tree. Sten glares at the empty horizon until his eyes water, the heat of the desert seeming to peel the earth from the sky. The days pass slowly, but with nothing to distinguish them they blur together like shadows in the sun.

Uzu walks so Sten can rest, but they do not talk. He returns to Lyssa when Sten wakes. No one points or shouts or cries or moans or judges Sten, even as they leave more and more of the People behind – a trail of bodies left to track their wandering way.

But the desert is not done with them, its final judgement marked one evening by dusty orange clouds on the horizon and death's taste in the air. It is not long before they hear the storm's shivering cry. It comes, shouting out its message, sending forth winds to whip up fangs of earth, and drawing a blanket of dust across the sky. Sten, walking alone, holds out his arms and screams up at the dark sky, willing it to take him, while around him the People scatter. They weep and hold their families and watch and wait to see who dies.

When the lightning comes, it separates the boiling dust and banishes the dark, a thousand jagged branches joining earth and sky.

Don't Dig Her Up Again

*Tom
Jordan*

Mags stared at the curtains and wondered if there would be an uptick in searches or even views directly after. It was almost all she could bring herself to think about in between the constant visits and the naps and the checkups.

She was able to talk through all the other stuff; the things that had happened, what she had thought, the things that she thought people had thought about her. It was expected, no matter how exhausting, with every single person she'd ever known coming through – final goodbyes, last minute confessions, old intrigues wrapped up in a bow.

When she was alone, well, what else was there left for her to do? She didn't have the attention or energy for books or movies let alone anything strenuous. Even the dying need their diversions.

The sound of someone cleaning downstairs. Humming and shuffling. It could be cleaning woman that Dee had hired or it could be one of their two daughters. 'Just popped in to see how you were doing, Mam.' Mags wasn't sure. How long had she been sitting there awake and contemplating? And then, a new thought – would they still watch her, she wondered.

She'd seen it with other girls, these massive, viral, postmortem spikes in interest, sometimes lasting for months or years. But, she had to remind herself, *they* were all a lot younger than her when they died and invariably, death was much kinder to them. It came out of nowhere and it was careful. It didn't drain them or mark them. It came quickly and took them whole.

And so they got to live on, unblemished and youthful while she sagged and the cancer spread out to her limbs.

The cleaner, or Caoimhe, or Lolly, whoever it was downstairs, had started hoovering. Mags smirked limply at the curtains – death was hot.

What was true of her life before her diagnosis was still true now. Dee and the kids were what was most important. She still preferred the white Kinder Bueno. Sex redeemed all.

This last felt even more apparent with her surroundings so drab and sterile, now that she could barely move by herself. She stared at the curtains hanging across from her that hadn't moved all day, that hadn't changed in years. Dull and grey and dusty. She'd have to point them out to Anastasia or was Yana her name, whoever it was downstairs, no she remembered it now. The nurse. The younger one, she'd be up again soon, she had said.

Mags sighed. The fatigue will become a bigger part of it all, the doctor had said, soon it'll overtake you out of nowhere.

It hurt her to know how she would leave this world, so drab and grey, especially at moments like this when she stacked it all up against the salacious burnouts of her younger rivals. No tabloid demise. No famous, abusive partners. No drugs. No rock and roll. No sex.

"'Completely hairless and bone-china pale," she died at home surrounded by loved ones, in the arms of her long-term partner…' the sentence trailed off to the back of her mind and away as a swoon of exhaustion built up inside of her. The curtains glimmered as her eyelids started to flutter.

·ılı· ·ıllı· ·ılı·

Mags had been dead for two weeks when the first cheque popped through the letterbox. Dee had never engaged with Mags' career beyond lending an ear from time to time so initially he assumed these checks were residuals from old scenes.

Eventually a friend told him about the videos. Stumbled across it, they said. How had he not known? Why, they asked, hadn't she told him? He was distraught.

·ılı· ·ıllı· ·ılı·

The nurse leaving woke her up. It was usually the case and it always unnerved her. How silent they could be running their tests. How little input was needed from her. How, having slept through the whole gamut of pricks and beeps, she still woke with a start when she felt them going. She had to stop herself from calling out. It wasn't the poor nurse's job to hold her hand.

The clock on her bedside locker read 6 p.m.; she focused on her breathing. People usually visited around now and Dee would be home from work soon but the wait felt interminable.

For the first time in her life the hours she spent alone had become the most difficult.

To distract herself, she took up her phone and googled her stage name. The first breaths came shallow as she waited for the page to load. The nurse had left the curtains open and the evening sun had gotten itself caught on one of their edges while making its way down for the night and the contrast of light and dark made that patch of grey look golden.

The search engine had finished its trawl and the page was ready and waiting as she pulled her focus from the window and started to tap. It was, as she expected, a full two pages of Google search before she managed to scroll past coverage of her illness – all tabloid carbon copies of the only two interviews she had given.

The journalists, one a young queer writer freelancing for a progressive publication and the other, an older male working on staff at a more centrist and established outfit, had both been lovely when she met them in person. They had been patient with her rambling and her forgetfulness and her tiredness. They had been understanding of the nurses and her friends coming and going and interrupting their time together. The younger writer was enthusiastic about her work and the older male was, at the very least, cognisant and respectful of her success.

She didn't have much energy for disappointment these days but she had been angry reading those "interviews". The first, by the younger writer, read half like a morbid interest piece and half like they were a provocative gonzo trying to humanise the freak that she was.

The older man had written effusively about "the unending, inescapable moment of imminent mortality," but any descriptions of her or her home and family had made them seem garish. She was a pretty corpse now, "bone-china pale," and not the "full blooded starlet on her knees or haunches some of us (though embarrassed to admit) might recognise." He put his readers at a distance from an illness like hers with the sort of life it was that he thought she had led, or at least, that's how Mags read it.

'You're being too harsh,' Dee had told her, but Dee was wrong.

Dee had always maintained that his connection with Mags and hers to him were stronger than those found and observed in other people's relationships because, unlike other people's, their love wasn't restrictive or limiting. It had always led to more; more experiences, more connections, more, well, more love. After she was gone, he would ask himself repeatedly, in the depths of his grief, how could something so boundless and fruitful not be worth the pain? It was, he told himself, over and over, it *was* worth it. How could it not be?

For a time after the revelation he felt like what Mags had done was to undermine all of that. He was angry. His moods began to swing from the pain of loss to the bitterness and resentment of the cheated and the deceived. It was easier at times, being bitter and resentful, but then when something reminded him of her, or he felt the urge to tell her something, or he passed someone with even the slightest resemblance to her, the pain returned and it was only doubled and it came with guilt on its back over the bitterness and resentment. The guilt crippled him worst of all.

◦╟◦ ◦╟╟◦ ◦╟◦

An old director of hers had seemingly read either one of the original hatchet jobs or one of the many shameless clickbait re-uploads and emailed her out of the blue to, what was it? 'Make sure she didn't want to get up on that pony one last time?' She had told him that she wished she had the energy but she had yet to respond to his subsequent reply – one sentence, 'What if you didn't need any energy?'

Lying in bed, the annoyance she initially felt came back to her. Why be so coy? she thought. What did he even mean?

◦╟◦ ◦╟╟◦ ◦╟◦

It was another six months after the revelation, nearly a full year after that first cheque when, on the same day, a parcel arrived at Dee's front door and a video file appeared in his intray.

The box was tattered. It had been handled roughly and, evidently, stored in a damp corner somewhere. He wondered if it had been forgotten and only lately remembered. It seemed strange and it annoyed him in that new way that things had never annoyed him before. She was dead, he thought, the least you can do is remember to deliver her fucking box.

◦╟◦ ◦╟╟◦ ◦╟◦

Mags had by now found one of her old videos on the kind of free to use website that she had spent her entire career railing against and she did not notice the sound of a car pulling up outside or the subsequent creak and thud of the front door opening and closing. Mags was totally submerged now, her focus flitting between the top half of the screen where her younger self clutched tight to a floppy purple dildo and grimaced threateningly past it into the depths of the camera, and the bottom half of the screen where the comments – each, she had to assume, typed one handed – were threaded below.

> **6911420:(x** : I wonder is she all pale and bald yet?
> Reply **bongobrains991:** I'd still fuck her probably.

The door to her bedroom was hardly ever closed these days. The nurses usually forgot it and she never had the energy to get out of bed just to close it herself. When she glanced up Dee was leaning against the door frame smiling at her.

'Hi darling,' he said.

'Hi baby.'

She switched off her phone.

'You're not watching dirty movies now are you?'

'Stop it,' she said, frowning at the blank screen.

Dee took two steps and gently sprawled himself out at the end of her bed like a child. He was nimble for his age and his weight came down softly. She tossed the phone away and took his body in whole – he was shifting slowly, getting comfortable – and still, after thirty years she marvelled at its brusque, angular grace.

'Ok,' he said, his words muffled by the duvet, eyes and fore-head now the only part of his face that she could see, 'How are you feeling?'

'No,' she said.

His eyes, bloodshot from screens all day at work, dull and warm and welcoming. She was taken by the urge to commit them to memory, as if that was all it took. Of all the things to lament, right at that moment it was them, somewhere between green and brown and gold and slightly reddened at the edges. She did not want them to be forgotten.

He rolled over with a groan so that he was looking at the ceiling.

'Ok, let me tell you about my day.'

'No,' she said, 'not that either.'

'Do you want a hug?'

It was then that she started to cry and Dee scrambled to embrace her.

'I don't want to die,' she said.

᛫ᚦ᛫ ᛫ᚦᚦ᛫ ᛫ᚦ᛫

Dee hadn't had sex in months and months, nearly over a year, in fact, if he ever took the time to stop and count it out, when the box and the video arrived. He had cut off any former lovers when Mags had become sick and had faithfully ignored any that had reached out since her death. He hadn't wanked in months either. He had, obviously, sworn off porn since the revelation, 'Necrophilliac,' he called it. 'Disgusting. Vile. Drivel.'

His friends knew not to bring up Mags' Last Hurrah (as they had taken to calling the video series when discussing it behind his back) and Dee knew it was best not to look for himself. Only pain, he decided, lay down that road. Even before, he hadn't liked watching Mags perform. It wasn't the same. It wasn't ever *really* Mags, or at least not his Mags.

He missed her, dearly, and bit by bit that feeling overtook any notion of betrayal. He came to understand why she'd done it, and had this not happened naturally he would have forced himself to because he still loved her as if he saw her every day. He decided that this would probably never change. He hadn't watched the videos yet and he thought that he probably never would, but enough time passed that they didn't enrage him as much as they once had.

That is to say, by the time that the box and the video arrived Dee had started to come to terms with it all.

Mags received another email from her old director.

'I'm serious,' it began, 'We can get you back up there and you won't have to lift a finger. And I promise I'll make you look amazing.'

She was lying in bed with Dee when the email arrived and he wanted to know what she was staring at.

'It's nothing,' she said.

That evening, the two of them still in bed together, she asked how he would feel if she performed again.

She continued staring at the phone in her lap while she asked him and his response was awkward and halting.

Memories interspersed between the two of them and bloated out, feeding on this discomfort. Different memories but similar. He thought about brushing the hair from her eyes and biting her lip; the feel of her legs straddling him on the outsides of his thighs, the weight of her pressing him to the couch. She thought about holding him down beneath her, how she would run her hand lightly across his chest and around his body, how it was ceaseless, always, always moving and how she wouldn't notice herself doing it until right at the end and then...

He asked her if she would be able to and she told him she would not.

'You miss it,' he said.

He leaned close in to hold her as he said this but the response it stirred up inside her was bilious and surprised her.

She snapped around to face him, pulling away in the process.

'It's not that,' she said. 'Can you *just* answer my question?'

'If it would make you happy.'

'If it would make me happy, what?'

She felt his gaze trace across her. Across the state of her.

The kids were on their way over. Every moment now was a diamond in the making, priceless and possibly exquisite but the pressure was suffocating. They just didn't have enough time for things like this. Dee left to get started on dinner.

When he was gone she took up her phone again and opened that latest email.

'How would this work?' she typed, and then sent.

The response was almost immediate.

'I can call you tomorrow to explain the details.'

The video file was untitled. Just a series of digits and letters. If it hadn't come from Mags' old email address he would have immediately disregarded it as a scam that had somehow slipped through Gmail's security features.

The file arrived nearly a half day before the parcel but it had remained unopened as seeing it had temporarily caused Dee to thrill with fear. His immediate reaction was to reach out to his daughters; his fingers trembled as he typed and then deleted a message.

He would get a similar feeling, only less intense, when by chance or really through some morbid curiosity he found himself scrolling through Mags' private social media pages. But the feeling seemed to belong to those cyberspaces and there was comfort there, like the quiet of a graveyard – it was bearable when he sought it out himself but petrifying now that it had caught him unprepared.

His stomach lurched. That old recognition – talking to her, being around her – she was there for an instant and when she disappeared he felt like he was plummeting. There was none of the distance afforded by her old posts and photos and captions and videos, a record of years that belonged firmly to the past.

(Received two minutes ago) – She was right there.

The fear passed quite quickly to become a strange and solemn weight which in turn passed as well so that the rest of his morning was spent too flustered and confused to commit himself to any one spot or activity. He floated mindlessly around the house until the arrival of the box that afternoon finally brought some clarity.

The postman standing oblivious at the door with the unannounced parcel in his hands made Dee think, or at least hope, that though he might not be privy to it, there was some sort of plan afoot, that someone (Mags?) was looking out for him.

⁂

The process was simple and painless. They would use old footage and images alongside new software to recreate her likeness and contort it in whatever ways you could possibly imagine. The contract would last two years. At best, she would live to see three months of those. After two years, the rights to her likeness would revert to Dee and it would be up to him what happens next. She hadn't told him. She wasn't sure how he would react or how she could make him understand – she signed the contracts while he was at work.

Discussions with the director and representatives from his production company along with her own ruminations had resulted in one extra condition that she had insisted upon but that her old director was only happy to agree to. This final element to the contract required photographs of her bedroom and kitchen and some particular old footage had to be found and sent over but it was easily arranged to have all this done while Dee was out of the house.

⁂

He opened the box and the first thing he saw was a note.

I'm sure I've missed you, it read, with a big confident *X* at the end. He recognised it from the notes he had received over a whole lifetime together but only began to save during her last few months, *Kids home tonight X. Can you remember to buy Weetabix this time… please? X.*

He held the card as if it was delicate and turned it over and over again but that's all it said, *I'm sure I've missed you.* He stared like it had taken decades to construct and still it might disappear in an instant, but the message didn't change.

The card was pastel pink. The ink was black. She had kissed it but it wasn't like the movies, the lipstick mark was faint and smudged, almost unrecognisable as a lipstick mark, completely unrecognisable as a mark that came from *her* lips.

It was a while before the box regained his attention. Its primary carriage was what looked like a helmet encased in foam padding and wrapped in soft, thin packing paper, all of which he let scatter about him to the floor along with the box as he took the helmet in his hands.

'Mags,' he whispered, 'What the fuck have you gone and done now?'

∿ ∿ ∿

There was nothing left for her to do. Somehow this last project had taken the pressure off. There were less panic attacks when she was alone. She found herself sleeping through the night again.

Those final few months were some of the happiest she ever had. Dee took time off work and the kids moved back home. They had breakfast together every day and dinner nearly every evening. It was like Chritsmas; they sat around and watched movies and they cooked and ate and drank and laughed. There was always the radio on or a speaker and the girls would dance and hold her by the hand and sometimes she even danced as well. Dee would take her by the hips. He'd charm her, constantly, and make her smile with his flirting and kiss her palms and cheek and feet and lips.

They would sit with her for hours and chat. One-on-one or all together, in every combination. They told her things that they had never told her, things they had hidden from her, things they thought would upset her, and all those little things that they had just never thought to share. It seemed so important now that nothing be left unsaid and she savoured every minute she spent listening to them. She was so proud.

Look at what you've done, she would marvel, look at this world you've had a hand in making.

It was still terribly sad and she was very afraid but Mags had never been so happy for so long when, surrounded by her loved ones, her two girls and her partner, she finally passed away. She never got to see any of the videos in the end. She died about a week before the first series of them had been completed. She had all but forgotten about them in the months since signing.

⫴ ⫼ ⫴

He thought about brushing the hair from her eyes and biting her lip. He could almost feel her legs straddling him on the outsides of his thighs, the weight of her pressing him to the couch. Ethereal, all phantom and pixel, but she still held him down beneath her. Her hands running lightly across his chest, around his body, ceaseless, never stopping for long enough for him to feel the press – he hardly ever noticed feeling them anyway.

The sound. He heard her whispers, close. Her lips tickled his ear, almost. He was lost in her. He felt himself getting more lost. He would always cry as he climaxed and he would sit there with her when he was finished. The scene was designed that way.

She would dismount and smile down at him. He would hear the smooch of a kiss on his forehead as she stooped and her long hair should have tickled his chest.

Then she would curl up next to him like a cat, telling him to 'find a pillow and cuddle up.'

'I miss you,' she'd say, 'and I can't hold you. But I'm right here baby and it's alright. You can go to sleep.'

Spectro

*Shane
Griffin*

'God painted the picture. We're just guessing what brush he used.' Jack was usually an outspoken atheist, but the girl he was trying to impress wore a crucifix, so I suppose he was flexible. It was a dumb line, but it seemed to work. I stifled a laugh and excused myself from the conversation.

The party was turning stale, a dry crust of physicists in conversation. I was an engineering student. Building things excited me more than edge cases and error margins. Jack's parties attracted a mix of disciplines, making them hit-and-miss for my romantic prospects. Murmurings from several competing discussions filled the apartment that night, allowing me to slip out under their din.

Jack's terrible chat-up line is the only thing I remember from my journey home. Maybe it stuck with me because of the alcohol. I can't be sure I didn't hit my head, and I don't think I took any narcotics. Perhaps I suffered a brief neurological episode, but whatever the cause, that stupid line bounced around my head. Before I stumbled back to my flat, I had a revelation.

A subset of my alcohol-saturated neurons started thinking about the nature of the universe. I'd always believed that time flowed linearly. One thing happened, and then the next thing happened. Like a series of photographs or frames of a movie, each moment existed and then didn't. Jack's silly image of God with a paintbrush inspired a thought experiment.

What if time worked like a painting? I thought of the beginning of time as a blank canvas. The first moment happened, the big bang, and God painted it. Then the next impossibly-thin-slice-of-everything occurred, and God painted that. At first, I thought God would need a new canvas for each moment, but that only led back to my old thinking. Instead, why not simply paint over the last picture?

As more came into existence, God added more paint. Layer upon layer of events, places, and people splashed on the canvas of our universe. Each instant becoming another masterpiece painted over the one before it.

Of course, God was only a convenient metaphor for the idea. I'd conceived a new way to think about the fourth dimension. The experiment concluded with the idea that every moment of history still existed, dormant under the surface of the present.

The more I thought about it, the more I felt the idea might have merit. Before I passed out that night, I convinced myself I could work out the mathematics of the cosmic artwork.

⑃⑂⑃

The following day, I woke up to a hangover which left me unable to ignore my heartbeat. My head pounded, and my breath fogged in the basement flat's stale air. Not the first Saturday morning that I had felt that deep chemical fear. Mrs Johnson lived upstairs. She started renting to me after her husband died. The flat was small and damp, but it suited my requirements. Apart from the cold, I loved that place.

I wrapped myself in my duvet and was shuffling towards the kitchenette when I remembered the cosmic painting. The theory recrystallised through my booze-induced anxiety, and I diverted to my desk to scribble out as much as I could remember. It spilled out so fluidly that I had the guts of the theory on paper by lunchtime. As hangovers go, it was one of my more productive ones.

The idea still made sense while sober, but it was so far from the accepted theory that I couldn't trust my mind. I needed an experimental basis to confirm my thinking. The principles of the idea lent themselves nicely to a design for a device that could show me an older layer of the universal painting. With no other weekend plans, I started building a time machine.

࿓ ࿓ ࿓

I worked night and day, exhausting myself and becoming a husk of a man by Monday morning. At that age, I could take the punishment. A couple of stereos and a camera had been sacrificed with no concrete result. I had built a machine, but it didn't do anything. My confidence remained sky-high, but I didn't have everything required to assemble a time machine, at least not lying around my flat. The project went on hold while I went to class and sourced the missing equipment.

The lecture hall was barely warmer than my basement. I can't remember the subject of the class. My mind refused to stay on topic, with the overhead projector a constant reminder of my unfinished project. After fifteen minutes, I realised I wasn't processing a word the professor said and gave up. I snuck out the back without drawing attention, knowing I would be academically and socially incompetent until I finished my machine. On my way out, I borrowed a projector from one of the electrical labs. It contained the parts I was missing. I'd have it back before anyone noticed, a few days, a week tops.

Three weeks later, I finally assembled the prototype of my machine. My flat looked like a junkyard, and my hygiene waned further by the day. I survived on a couple of hours of sleep each night. Besides swift resupply missions, I spent all my waking time on my machine. I lived alone, but I suspected my lifestyle was attracting rodents. Intermittent noises distracted me. I ignored the scratching and focused on my work, unable to find the exact source.

It was late when the machine was ready for its first test. Dim orange light dripped through the windows, which I blocked with pillows. The only other light came from the screen, where I typed out the run command. I pressed the enter key, and the room lit up.

The machine screeched to life, producing a sound like a dozen angry bats attacking a beehive. I stepped back towards the door, fearing the thing would explode. Instead, off-white light burst from the modified overhead projector, which sat atop the monstrosity. A rectangular portion of the back wall lit up with the barest hint of blue, and the machine settled into a pleasant hum as though the bees had won.

Overall the experience was underwhelming. The light from the projector was supposed to catch an older layer of the cosmic painting and cast it on my wall. All I saw were the shadows of my furniture. It wasn't unexpected. The first test was always bound to fail, but my gut sank nonetheless. I was about to shut the device off and get some sleep when I noticed something odd. A shadow that shouldn't be there.

It was subtle, just a dark bump rising from the shadow of my bed. I threw the duvet to the floor, but the mysterious shadow remained. The shadow of my duvet was still there too.

I could hear my heartbeat again. I upended the bed without a care for where it landed and shoved everything I could into a corner to make space in the tiny flat. Even with all of the furniture cleared, the shadows remained.

They were blurry and dark, but the outlines of my bed and locker were still on the wall. The machine worked. The silhouettes were from a scene that no longer existed. The telltale bump must have been me sleeping in the bed. It must have been recent, considering how well the shadows lined up.

I celebrated with a warm beer and a cigarette, admiring my achievement, the world's first chrono-spectrograph, splitting the light of another time. Excitement kept me awake long enough to take photographs and notes of the experiment. When I ran out of observations, I shut the machine down and passed out on the pile of bedding in the corner.

Waking the following morning, I couldn't wait to resume work on the project. I should have drafted a thesis and started to look for financial backing, but I couldn't pull myself out of creative mode. The fuzzy shadows of my bed were nowhere near the definition I had hoped. If I could improve the machine, it would prove the theory for me. Some other sap could write it up and get their name in a journal.

I'd been away from college for three weeks without plans to return. A Nobel Prize was more enticing than a bachelor's degree. My machine could revolutionise historical research and solve crimes moments after they happened. With a little more time, I was sure I'd solve the problems with my design. I could change the world if my machine could produce something more than shadow puppets.

I committed the entirety of myself. Time passed in a blur of repetitive incremental experiments. My hair grew well past anything stylish, and my pallor increased similarly. Deep and hollow mildew odours emanated from every corner of the flat. Mrs Johnson was too deaf to be bothered by the racket I made every night. She would have evicted me on the spot if she had any idea of the state of the place.

The scratching noises increased as I ignored my chores. I set traps, but whatever caused the noise didn't bite. Feral instincts took over as I became a singularly focused hermit. My decay became the price of daily progress. Each failure brought me closer to my goal, even if I had to invent new forms of logic to explain them.

⑈⑈ ⑈⑈⑈ ⑈⑈

A few weeks after the first experiment, I had another brush with success. It was late at night. All my breakthroughs came when the rest of the world had gone to sleep. A new image beamed against the back wall in crisp full colour. Under the machine's pleasant drone, I stared at myself, asleep in a bed that wasn't there anymore.

The picture was clear and vibrant, a perfect slice of cosmic artwork. Exactly what I predicted the machine could do. I took photographs of the first high-definition spectrograph and noted the machine's configuration.

Rerunning the experiment confirmed my results, so I began to look further back in time. Increasing the power peeled back more layers of cosmic paint, but changing the configuration required several minutes of computation. The basement didn't have a very long history, having been excavated about a century before I moved in. Everything above a certain power level resulted in a kind of dark and bumpy nothingness, which I took to be the earth which had once filled the space.

I noted the upper limit and dialled the power down incrementally. The next set of experiments produced scenes of a coal bunker, which must have been the basement's original purpose. One showed a man shovelling coal, accompanied by a small white dog. I took photographs of that experiment as it was the first time I had seen a historical person other than myself.

After the coal bunker, the basement became storage. Years flew by with each experiment, though very little changed. My machine showed me boxes of Christmas decorations that would move about the picture as I ran tests. It was so dull that it was easy to forget I was viewing raw images of the past. Still, I noted down everything I saw in case any of it turned out to be significant.

Outside, days turned into nights and back into days, but no light breached my basement laboratory. In the darkness, time became ironically meaningless. Perfect black could fill the basement in one moment when my machine suddenly lit the room like a summer's day.

I made token efforts to clean the flat. The mess was getting in the way of the experiments, and the scratching seemed constant. I knew I would have to groom myself and find someone to present my work to, but I was determined to document the basement's complete history first.

The next time I saw people in a projection, there was a man in a velvet suit with a woman in a turquoise cocktail dress. She leaned across some boxes, and he had his trousers around his ankles. I stared at the unexpectedly revealed secret and wondered what led them to use my basement for their rendezvous. They looked away from the projector, denying me their identities.

I didn't know Mrs Johnson's age or how long she had owned the property. The woman hunched over those boxes could have been my landlady. Whoever they were, I had intruded on a private moment. For the first time, I wondered if my machine could do more harm than good. Who knew if their affair was still a secret? I took some notes but skipped the photographs. It wouldn't have been decent. The image still lit up the back wall when I heard a knock on my door.

My brain seized. It had been so long since someone knocked on my door that the sound seemed alien. A second knock came, forcing instinct to take over. I pulled the plug on my machine and tossed my duvet over it. The visitor wasn't likely to react well to the vintage pornography splayed across my wall, and I planned on keeping my invention a secret.

I opened the door to find Jack holding a box of beer.

'So you're alive,' he said. 'You look like shit. Are you ok?'

'Hey,' I glanced over my shoulder to confirm my secrets were safe. Jack was one of the few people I knew who could understand what I was doing. 'I'm fine, just been busy. What's up?'

'We missed you last night. Where have you been?'

'I've been here. What was last night?'

'The party! How did your exams go?'

It took me a moment to realise I had just missed an entire semester. Jack took the opportunity to slip past me and invite himself in.

My silence was enough for him to figure out what I was thinking. 'Oh no! Seriously? You didn't sit your exams?'

'I haven't been on campus in months.'

'Really? I could have sworn I saw you at lunch a few weeks ago.'

'I've barely left this flat since that party at your place. The one with all the physicists and that religious girl.'

'Mary? If she asks, you haven't seen me.'

'I haven't seen you. That's the point!'

Jack placed the beer on my two-seater kitchen table and sat down. 'That was months ago. Why don't you tell me what you've been up to?' He took out two bottles and handed one to me. I accepted the beer and cleared some clothes off the other chair to sit down.

'You first!'

⊪· ⊪⊪· ⊪·

Two hours and six bottles later, I was all caught up on Jack's latest conquests and adventures. He had a lot to say, but I had

189

trouble paying attention. From what I managed to glean, Mary had been showing up at his apartment every other Sunday, and he was considering moving. I kept my eyes on the beer, afraid I would reveal something by looking back at my machine. I could feel the alcohol chipping away at my restraint. A gnawing part of me wanted to share everything I had discovered. If only to have Jack confirm I hadn't gone mad.

Jack was either polite enough not to mention the mess or oblivious to it. Neither of us acknowledged the scratching sounds, which persisted. Jack was curious about my absence but subtle enough not to force me into a lie. He let me drink and get comfortable, building up a debt of conversation before asking me to repay.

'So, what have you been doing down here?' He opened another beer and slid it across the table. 'And what are you hiding under that blanket?'

I accepted the drink, along with the fact that I was about to spill the beans. During my months of work, I never bothered to come up with a cover story, and I failed to think of one on the spot. I liked Jack, and I owed my idea to his daft line. I scribbled out a non-disclosure agreement on a coffee-stained scrap of paper. It wouldn't hold up in court, but it made a point.

'Seriously?'

I nodded, and he signed with barely a hint of resentment.

Jack was a quick study. After another beer, he had his head around the basic concept of peeling back time. He read my notes quietly and only stopped to ask about symbols and phrases I had invented.

'Wild,' he said, putting the last page down. 'It's a novel idea. The maths works, but no one will fund that research.'

'I don't need money. Not for that anyway.' I nodded towards the duvet-covered mystery.

'No…' he stood, realising what I was hiding. 'No way!'

I crossed the room and yanked the duvet away, upending it with modest showmanship.

Jack kept his reserve but stepped quickly to inspect my work. I let him give the apparatus a good once-over.

'Alright,' he said. 'Assuming this isn't an elaborate ruse, that looks like a time machine. Either way, you are a better engineer than I thought.'

'You said the maths works. Just watch.' I loaded the parameters of a previous experiment. After a few seconds of screeching, the back wall lit up to show the man shovelling coal with his little dog.

Jack inspected the image, darting his eyes between the wall and the machine. 'Got a pen?'

'Sure. Why?'

'Because… I have an idea.'

We spent the next few hours working through formulas and refining the mathematics of time. The beer ran out, so we switched to coffee. Jack asked questions and took notes. I worried we might run out of notepads. Morning arrived around the same time we finished up.

'I need to go,' Jack said, holding a stack of paper. 'This should help. I think. I'm tired, but it might be a game changer.'

'Thanks,' I replied. 'But I'm not splitting the Nobel with you.'

'Ha, see if it works first! I'm going to visit my parents for a couple of weeks. I wrote their number down somewhere in there. Call me if you get stuck.'

'Will do. Thanks!' I closed the door behind him and regressed into a zombified state. Months of research and development had been rough, but a night of drinking and talking had drained my tank. I pulled the duvet from the floor and wrapped myself in it. Jack's notes made good bedtime reading. I should have brought him on board sooner.

॥‧ ॥‧ ॥‧

Jack's ideas were surprisingly easy to incorporate into my machine. All I required was a shift in my thinking, having all the materials already scattered throughout my flat. My original design worked, but it wasn't as ambitious as it could have been. The device peeled back layers of cosmic artistry and projected the result on a surface. Jack realised there was no reason to limit the projection to two dimensions.

Modifying the device was simple. I had over-engineered the damn thing, so I spent a few hours pulling bits out. Every other leap forward had taken weeks, but time machine version two was up and running before dinner.

I input the parameters of my favourite experiment and started the improved device. The brain-grating screech remained, but once the machine warmed up, an image appeared in the room. No longer was it a simple picture projected against the wall, but a scene inside the room. The coal shoveller and the little dog shimmered as apparitions standing in my basement flat. A three-dimensional hologram of a man who must have been dead fifty years, projected where he once stood.

Jack's enhancements revealed a previously unknown dimension. My machine wasn't simply peeling back the layers of space-time. It was allowing me to slip between them. Watching the blue-hued character was overwhelming. I giggled, thinking it was funny that I had gone straight to 3D and skipped video. Live playback might have been possible with more projectors and processing power. That could wait.

I had one more notepad left to fill. The experiment needed to be repeatable, so I shut the machine down and spun it up again. The same parameters produced the same ghostly man and dog. I noted down the success.

I should have stopped. I lived in squalor, and my bank account was drying up. I needed to shower and shave. I had so many reasons to stop. My notes were enough for a write-up in any scientific journal, and the machine was ready for its debut.

Still, I wanted to keep my secret for a little bit longer. I decided to run through all my previous tests with the new enhancements. From the coal man up to the present, I wanted to confirm the entire history of my flat. I configured another experiment and fired up the machine.

This time there was no man or dog, only the coal bunker. I took notes, set the next power level, and restarted the machine.

The image skipped a couple of years. The coal bunker was gone, leaving the room empty, apart from dust and a little gravel. I took my notes and moved on to the next timestamp.

The boxes were back, now scattered across the floor. I knew they were present for most of the basement's history. Shimmering waves covered the floor, and it took me a moment to figure out that the basement had flooded. A fresh historical discovery which I noted before moving on.

It wasn't long before I caught up with the couple in their party attire. I had forgotten about them after the night of drinking with Jack. The possible exploitation of my invention scared me. My machine could be a problem in the wrong hands. I moved to shut down the experiment but paused before I could flick the switch. There were so few people in any of the projections. The scene was made interesting by their presence alone, but I was also curious about who they were and why they'd had their affair in my basement.

The man was too close to the wall to get a good look at him. The woman's head looked towards the door, and I had to squeeze up by the wall to see her face. She wasn't Mrs Johnson. Her eyes were too far apart, and she was far too pretty. She gawped back at me with an open mouth, a look of guilt and surprise.

I shut the machine down and took a note not to rerun that experiment again. There was no scientific value in disturbing the couple any further. I also noted to be careful where I ran experiments in the future out of fear of embarrassing myself.

The next set of experiments yielded little of interest. The boxes shifted positions over the years, more crumpled and worn than before. I made brief notes and moved on, waiting for something to change. My earlier experimental series had stopped when Jack arrived, so I was moving into unknown territory.

Soon the boxes were gone. The basement must have sat unused for some time before Mrs Johnson started renting to me. I knew what to expect after I moved in, and it wouldn't interest even the most anoraked historian. I was about to stop for the night and get some sleep, but before I shut down the device, I noticed an anomaly.

A patch of space shimmered, unlike everything around it. I was surprised I even noticed the subtle disturbance. It was a thin haze, about five and a half feet tall, which I couldn't explain. I started scribbling out a new page of notes, but it was hard to describe apart from its dimensions.

I took photos to go with my meagre descriptions and repeated the experiment. The anomaly appeared again. I shut the machine down and checked it for problems. When I reran the test, the disturbance returned.

The anomaly was so unexpected that I could have missed it in previous trials. I reset for an earlier experiment and fired the machine up again. The boxes returned, but to my disappointment, the anomaly did not. The preceding months overflowed with discoveries, and the disturbance felt like it would be the last secret revealed in that basement. Sleep clawed at me. Through a yawn, I caught a shimmer in the corner of my eye.

The disturbance was there, a few feet left of its original position. Whatever it was, it could move. I noted its location and resumed my experimental trials. The thing was easy to spot once I knew how to find it. It moved around the room but was present in all of my tests. A few experiments more, and I caught up on scenes of myself moving in. My clutter made the thing harder to spot, but invariably I found the patch of space unlike any other somewhere in the room.

Explanations for the shimmering almost-something eluded me, and I resolved to tell Jack about it in the morning. I had photographs and detailed notes to share with him. The basement had little else to show me, and my need for sleep was becoming immediate. Before I crawled into my makeshift bed, there was one last thing I wanted to try. Someone was bound to take a photograph standing beside their own historical doppelganger. I decided to be the first.

⑊⑊⑊

Holding as still as possible for fifteen minutes gave me an aching jaw and a sore arm, but it was worth it for a clear image in the projection. I set my camera on a timer and configured my machine with its lowest power setting.

The device screeched to life and flooded the basement with its eerie light. I dashed to my second position and held still, only relaxing when I heard the camera click. I looked to my right to confirm my doppelganger had appeared correctly. He was there, and he looked terrible. As I inspected the wildness of his hair, I noticed someone else. I wasn't alone with myself.

A woman was standing on the opposite side of my double, hiding behind his dressing gown and general dishevelment. I stumbled back and fell over the edge of my desk. No woman stood there when I posed for the photo, but one was there now. She shimmered with the same blue hue as my other self, a part of the projection. Explanations collided through my brain, but the only viable one was the machine had pulled an artefact from another layer of time.

Time froze while I got my feet back under myself. I sidled around the room, keeping one eye on the door. Cold sweat rolled down my back. Curiosity pulled me to look closer, but half of my body prepared to bolt.

The woman was familiar. Her turquoise cocktail dress marked her as the lady from the affair, but she looked different. Her jaw sloped to one side, dislodged and bruised. Her hair was dark and slick, matted to the side of her head. She stood beside my doppelganger, staring intently at the side of his head. With her jaw hanging, she seemed to bare her teeth. I dared to move closer. Before I could find my courage, she moved first. Her neck twitched.

My heart stopped. I felt sure I was dead, but it came thumping back so loud I feared the ghost would hear it. The woman turned her head in my direction but didn't seem able to see me. She wasn't an artefact or a mistake generated by my machine.

My mind raced. The device was supposed to peel back layers of space-time and show what lay beneath. Jack's changes made it project the dimension between those layers. Somehow the woman in the turquoise dress was there, existing outside the moments of time.

I watched, not daring to move or make a sound. She only cared about my doppelganger. She swiped her whispy arm through his dopey grin and seemed disappointed by the lack of response. She turned away, flinging her arms wildly. Her evident frustration grew until her nails struck the air like a solid wall. Under the thumping of my heartbeat, I heard scratching.

I covered my ears. The noise grew louder, and the space where the woman clawed started to glow. The disturbance grew bigger and brighter until it swallowed her, and the sound stopped.

She was gone, leaving behind a subtle shimmering nothingness in the projection. She was still there, of course. I knew she hadn't gone anywhere, only moved on to the next place between moments. One step closer to the surface of the painting.

॥|· ·|||||· ·|||·

I don't remember much of what happened after that, except for the fire. An unrelenting compulsion to destroy everything and pretend it never happened. The basement burned quickly. I think I made an effort to alert Mrs Johnson. I hope she made it out in time.

I never heard from Jack again. He didn't have a copy of my notes, and I left everything of my old life behind. I still fear he will recreate my work, but not as much as I fear the damned scratching.

This Is About Art

Poppy Sheridan

Upstairs, in the Pompidou Centre in Paris, there is a large white canvas. It is completely blank, free from any marks or blemishes. It has no frame. It takes up an entire wall, the stretch of its surface hanging placidly in place, towering quietly over anyone who walks past. The ripples of its woven face sit underneath a thin wash of clear varnish, and as the sunlight from a nearby window moves slowly around the room, the strands of linen that make up its surface rise and fall in a micro-dance of shadow and highlight.

On the other walls in the room hang several more complex pieces. One canvas is completely covered in an uneven layer of pale blue paint, while another has a thick black line drawn diagonally from one corner to the other. A fourth painting is made up of hundreds of tiny squares scattered in a myriad of colours across a cream background. They stand in a silent assembly, stretched imposingly from ceiling to floor, the colours of their surfaces reflecting pastel recreations on the polished wooden floorboards.

But the white canvas stands out by virtue of how completely unremarkable it is.

ıⅠ‖· ılⅡ‖ı· ıⅠ‖·

I am seven and I have won an art competition. I did a drawing of some horses running in a field, and I have been invited to go to Dublin for a prize ceremony. Dad takes me on the train from Cork to Dublin, and my Granny comes too. On the train, he proudly explains to us why my piece has won. It is the story behind it, he says, the fact that you can see horses coming in and out of the picture, it makes you think about the world beyond the drawing. I listen carefully, nodding along with what he says. I didn't mean to make it like that when I was drawing it, but I am glad that's what I did.

On the way back home, I open my prize. It is a case filled with art supplies. There are oil pastels in twenty different colours, there are paints and paintbrushes, and there are colouring pencils and a drawing pad. I turn the oil pastels over in the case, reading the names written on the side, names like "burnt sienna" and "ultramarine". I have never heard of these colours before, and I want to scribble on the pad to see what they will look like.

Dad stops me from taking them out. He tells me that this is a special set, that it's not for just messing around, that I am allowed to draw one picture now, and that's it. I carefully use the pencils to draw two dogs in a kitchen. They are both wagging their tails.

When I go home, I carefully put the case under my bed. I leave it there, unsure of what event will be important enough for me to use it.

When I am twelve, I pull it out and the paints have gone mouldy.

ıⅠ‖· ılⅡ‖ı· ıⅠ‖·

When I first saw the white canvas in the Pompidou, I hated it. At the age of twelve, I felt it represented everything I despised about modern art. Canvas was made to be filled with works that proved the skill of the artist, not left empty. As far as I could see, paintings where the artist had put in almost no effort were selling for millions of dollars around the world, and there seemed to be no place for simple realism anymore.

At home, I had a children's introductory book to the great Renaissance painters, and I had poured over their drawings, studying the deft skill with which they created lifelike images out of nothing. I knew that was the real mark of an artist, the ability to study the world around you and reproduce beautiful versions of it using nothing but your own hands.

I was very young, but I still believed that I knew enough about art to declare the white canvas to be rubbish, and move on.

⫴ ⫼ ⫴

I am thirteen and I am trying a new method of using watercolours that I have seen on YouTube. I have watched videos of artists creating works with incremental washes of paint, letting each layer dry before going over the painting with new colours. With each wash they are so precise in where the paint goes, ensuring that every brushmark is a carefully calculated movement in the communication of shape. I am enchanted by how each blanket of colour changes the appearance of the picture, and how beautiful and defined the finished works are.

I place an apple on the table in front of me and begin. I meticulously lay down a layer of pale red in an apple-shape and then sit excitedly, waiting for it to dry. The paint mattifies and the shine of the water disappears, and I know it is time for the next layer. This time I put down a layer of dark yellows and reds, watching how shadows and hues begin to develop, and the sharp shape of the apple's skin begins to emerge. By the time my final layer is completed, a carbon copy of the apple sits on my page, delicate and light.

Dad comes over to have a look. He says it looks like an apple, but that's it, and it makes no sense to use watercolours this way. He grabs my paintbrush from me and my muscles tense. Look, he says, ripping the page with my apple out of my sketchbook, this is how you do it, he says, this is what watercolours were made to be used for. He soaks the page in water and then starts smearing reds and yellows across it, allowing them to bloom into each other in one crude layer. He pushes each colour expertly in the direction that he wants it to go, and the result is something that looks like an apple, but is also bolder and more demanding, its dense colours and expanding shape exhausting the eye.

He throws the brushes down and says 'You see, what's the point in using watercolours like the way you were doing, this is how you're supposed to do it, I want to see you doing it like this from now on.'

After he leaves I sit in silence. Then I start painting.

I try to do it correctly, but the colours always bleed out.

As I grew, I realised that my earlier decisions to gauge the value of a painting by its realism was a childish mistake. I began to take note of the emotion a piece elicits from the viewer and the stylised nature of elements such as brushstrokes and colour choices.

Around the age of fifteen, I became obsessed with a painting by Jack B. Yeats that hung on the first floor of the Crawford Gallery in Cork City. It was called *A Race in Hy Brazil*, and it depicted a fantasy island, similar to Tír na nÓg, with people lining up with their horses preparing to race. Surrounded in an ornate gold frame, the painting was a lavish construction of aggressive slashes of oil paint, the vibrant blues and yellows coming together to create something that just about resembled figures. I would disappear into the Crawford as often as I could to stare at it, mesmerised by the sculptural effects of the brushstrokes, and the borderline nonsensical colours. What struck me the most about the experience of viewing the painting was how my mind would empty of any analytical impulse when I looked at it; I was simply happy to be enchanted by every golden fold of sky and every navy swirl of grass.

I discovered that other works were having similar effects on me, despite their abstract nature. I became fascinated with any Rothko that I stumbled across, the large shapeless smudges of colour looming over me in a warm intimidation. My favourite Renaissance work had become Donatello's wooden carving of the Penitent Mary; I studied photos of the work, tracing the shadows cast by the rough edges of her miserable face, exhilarated by how something so crude could evoke such deep despair. I still had no time for the basic contemporary pieces that had been taking space in the halls of Modern Art museums, but I was beginning to realise that there were other things to art besides rigidly adhering to proportion and perspective.

I am fifteen and I am practising pencil sketches for my Junior Cert art exam. I draw a crumpled bottle, looking at every curve and crack in the plastic, trying to pay attention to where the light hits the transparent material. I use a graphite pencil, leaning heavily on the lead to indicate where shadows are present.

When I am finished Dad looks at it. He says it is flat. I don't really understand what he means. He tells me that my shading isn't good enough, and my lines are too light and shaky to convey shape properly. He takes his own pencils from the good drawer upstairs and proceeds to draw a quick sketch to illustrate his point. His lines are strong and sure and harsh, and when he is finished the contours of his work leave deep grooves in the paper.

I nod as if I understand, and I try again. I stare at plant pots and CD cases and tupperwares, filling page after page, trying to capture the drama of their form. I bring them all back to Dad, but he says they are all flat, and he says he doesn't understand why I continue to draw them like this. Each time I go back to try again, my lines become shakier, and the thudding in my ears becomes louder.

The next weekend he takes me to see one of his colleagues, as he believes I need a more directive force with my work. They study my sketchbooks together, discussing the issues with my drawings, and agreeing that yes, it is very flat, and none of the images I produce come across as particularly interesting. I stand in the corner nodding, quietly panicking because I do not understand what else I am supposed to be doing.

⎪⎪· ⎪⎪⎪⎪· ⎪⎪·

Despite this newfound love of pieces that worked their way past the basic foundations of reality, I still disregarded the more conceptual, contemporary pieces. If I walked through a gallery that contained brutalist collages or installations of everyday objects strewn around the floor, I would pick my way haughtily past them, considering them to be shallow and worthless. When looking for inspiration for my own work, I was still looking for artists that utilised *skills*, and while I accepted the Impressionists and the Cubists for their strange takes on perception, anything beyond that was simply a shallow grab for attention.

It was when I was eighteen, and made aware of *Fountain* by Marcel Duchamp, that my stance crumbled. *Fountain* was nothing more than a mass produced urinal that Duchamp purchased and then anonymously submitted for a 1917 exhibition of the *Society of Independent Artists*. It was not received well, and the curators hid the piece behind a partition during the exhibition, perhaps due to a fear that it would offend the visiting audiences. But Duchamp had never intended the work to be pleasing to the eye; it was made to make people *think*, to reject the classical ideal of art as a visual and emotional pleasure. In submitting the urinal for exhibition, he wanted his audience to engage with the cerebral and question the strict guidelines that had come to define art; what is truly so low-brow about the smooth curves of a mass-produced porcelain urinal, besides our own belief that there are certain processes of the human body that we should not have to acknowledge? The result of this piece was a cosmic shift in the art world, where people began to rethink the pedestal they had placed artistic labour and propriety on.

Learning about this event was the final straw needed to destroy my arrogant disdain of non-traditional art. I finally saw that controversy had value, that only by aggressively ripping through the conventions we wrap around ourselves could we move into new eras of creation. I began to take a new look at works that I had always hated. Tracey Emin's installation *My Bed* now felt like an intriguing statement on the residue of life. Damian Hirst's bisected cows both horrified me and made me wonder why humans can be so determined to mystify the biology of a body to the point that they reject any opportunity to be faced with its fascinating reality. I had found a new way of looking at art, and therefore the world: I wanted to look at the things people had done and ask *why* they had done them, and what my initial revulsion could tell me about myself. The boundaries of what the world could be had been broken open, and the possibilities felt fresh and exciting.

⫼⫼⫼

I am sixteen and I am drawing a bag of flour. It is eight o'clock in the evening when I begin. I draw in coloured pencil, sticking to a strict palette of yellow, orange and blue. I do not focus on the bag as a whole, but instead I pick apart all the individual triangles, squares and pentagons that make up the crumpled paper of the bag. I isolate each shape, assign it a colour, and then fit them together like stars. I finish at two o'clock in the morning. My neck is aching.

Dad is up and I show him the finished drawing. He is delighted and tells me that this is the closest I have come to producing real art. I keep the picture of the flour bag safe in a plastic folder in my room.

⫼⫼⫼

Like many self-obsessed teenagers on the verge of adulthood, my standard for what defined art was set very high. I would consider the effort and thought that had gone into a piece and whether it could bring out any emotional response in the viewer. I would consider whether it possessed any damning statements about the world, or whether if by looking through it we could understand ourselves in new ways. I praised Van Gogh for making us question what colour really was, I spent hours staring at the works of Kandinsky, trying to understand what his feather-light squares were really saying. I poured over my father's modern furniture books, fascinated by the artists who were trampling the lines between a usable form and a useless beauty.

As I questioned the works around me, I was also forced to question my own work. I had always been praised for my strikingly realistic depictions of the world around me, but I began to feel that this could not possibly be enough. I would stare at what I'd drawn and feel nothing. I went through every piece I'd ever created – paintings of flowers, charcoal sketches of my classmates, ridiculous experiments with oil paints – and deemed them all worthless. I could finally see them for what they were: deadened copies of the world around me, with nothing new to say about the experience of living.

⊪ ⊪⊪ ⊪

I am seventeen and I am sitting across from my therapist. She is gently questioning me about my home life, trying to get to the root of why I have developed a habit of trying to hurt myself when I am left alone. I am impatient with the questions about my parents and

I want to move onto more important things, but she keeps pushing for more stories.

I tell her a story about when I was eight, and I entered into a local art competition to design a poster for Fota Wildlife Park. I drew some butterflies flying around a giraffe and wrote "Come see our magical world" in big glittery letters. I didn't win. I showed it to Dad and he said that of course you didn't win, there's nothing special or interesting about it, all you've done is drawn some but-terflies and poured some glitter on it, what did you expect. The next year I entered the same competition and drew a more ornate scene, with zebras and cheetahs and tigers and emus dotted over a bright savannah. I won first prize.

I glance up at my therapist and she is looking at me. She asks me if I think this is an appropriate way to speak to a child. I don't want to think about the answer.

Later on, Dad has to pick me up from therapy, because Mum gets stuck at work. On the way home he tells me that he doesn't do empathy and is just going to let Mum deal with me. I sit next to him, watching the rain spatter the windscreen, and feel the familiar sensation of my skin cells crawling over each other to hide inside my bones.

ıļı· ·ıļļı· ·ıļı·

The stringent requirements I had put in place to define art be-came overwhelming. I felt so lost, incapable of creating any-thing without being aware of how useless it was. I wanted so much to shake the complicated, elitist definitions that I had created for myself, and go back to when the simple act of dragging a coloured pencil across a sheet of paper made me feel pure delight. But every time I opened my sketchbook, I would feel the fingers of my thoughts shove themselves into the soft tissue of my brain, taunting me with how useless my work was, how simplistic my designs were, how unoriginal and sickening they looked on the page.

As the years wore on, the white canvas crawled its way back into my brain. I found myself returning to it day after day, analysing it from every angle, trying to understand it. I desperately wanted to know how something so simple could be allowed to take up space, how its mere existence as a canvas permitted it to sit in comfortable silence alongside its more complex peers.

Slowly I realised that art goes beyond the efforts of the artists and the reactions it provokes. It is wholly independent of the human life that swarms around it, and the opinions of the masses cannot alter the simple fact of its presence on earth. It is art because it exists, and it exists only for its own sake.

Nearly a decade on from when I first saw the white canvas, I realised that it is not only art, but art in its purest form.

⫶⫶⫶ ⫶⫶⫶⫶ ⫶⫶⫶

I am twenty and I haven't picked up a pencil in more than a year. I can feel my carefully cultivated skills slipping away from me, and I am terrified that if I try to begin again I will be incapable of drawing even the simplest thing. The world around me is screaming at me, the sky wants to be painted, the bus shelter across from me wants me to capture how its gleaming silver railing contrasts against the dark hills. My hands shake. I think of my father, sitting miles away, alone in our small kitchen, his worn-out body wrapped in blankets. A lump rises in my throat.

I am twenty and I do not know what I am. I am an artificial girl, someone else's creation. The world wraps around me and doesn't tell me what it wants. I dress like my friends in order to provide myself with some semblance of an identity. I get lost in cities where the sheer magnitude of people is enough to overcome my fragile sense of self.

I want to be a white canvas I want to be clean and unblemished I want to be empty I want to be nothing and still be enough I want to sit in front of it for years until it swallows me up and I can hang in a corner while people walk past me without a second thought.

Please do not paint me I am tired and I cannot hold anymore colours.

Birthday

Maria
O'Brien

A sharp flex of my wrists and *The Times* billows out, a grand sail puffed in the summer breeze, a buoyant buffer between me and beyond. Let's see. *Carbon emissions... Big tech firm opens... Hotel skyline...* Is this last week's rag? Last year's? Nicer to sit with it rather than actually read the thing. Maybe I'll have a fag. There's time – time for all on a Sunday in Dublin. What a beautiful, bountiful day is Sunday. The longest of the days because nothing is planned. Nothing *has* to be. And time is less of a construct than a feeling. Yes, I can agree with that now that the big birthday is looming. *Looming.* The word would suggest terror. Am I afraid? Old Father Time never deluded me. I knew this day would come. It came as it always said it would, no faster or slower than expected. No, that's not true. It has come too fast altogether. But here it is, like it said it would be, and there's no arguing to be had. No one to argue with. Restrain the monologues! *Supreme Court rules... Will Ireland keep the crown?* What's more, I'm not in the mood for arguing. I feel exceptionally light actually. Eau de parfum Merrion Square is enlivening. Here on my bench, grand trees gather around, flashy hordes of tulips kissing their feet with big red fleshy lips. Wouldn't mind growing old if pretty things like that still flocked. *Still* – as though someone is listening. Life is a play, as the good man said. Life is this heavenly smell. Breath deep old boy, just like at the seaside.

What noise though. An incessant propulsion grinding away. Like a giant bee. Sounds like a… yes, a lawnmower. Quite the undercover agent, surreptitiously peeping between my hat and broadsheet. *We meet again, Mr Bond.* Strange, he's not mowing straight, winding this way and that in his luminous cap. There are people watching. Some sort of show. Art al fresco. What a racket. I'd say he's pleased with himself too, look at me and my idea – came straight from my head you know. So he mows some shape into the lawn, and what? It must fade in a few weeks. Transitory, I suppose. The rule of demand for rarity as Mr Hanlon would say, decent boss that he was. Come see it now! When it's gone, it's gone! What a fast world we live in. I prefer the things that remain. The eternal things. The ancient statues of empires long perished still standing, still wanted.

Can't read with it. Best stroll on away before that light feeling fades. It's still good and early, there will be another spot. Not as good as that spot, but another. Good to stretch the legs anyway. Get stiff so quickly these days. Not as sprightly as that robin. Show off. There's always a robin hopping about Merrion. Probably not the same robin, but possibly. It could be the same robin. It could be the same robin I've been seeing since I was a boy, I guess. How would I know the difference. That's a charming thought. A little pal. They say robins are passed souls come to visit. How does it go? *When robins appear, loved ones are near* – that's it. Reincarnation, the ultimate loophole. Does that mean I'll become a robin too? What about the other birds? I'd rather be a falcon, of course, if I could choose. Now who is the show off. Good to smile, even if it's at one's own jokes. Seems a lonely sort of thing, but it isn't.

Now up it would be a shame to sit back down. I'll pop outside to the art fair along the railings, keep up the momentum. Good for the mind to experience new things. That's why Marianne went to so many evening classes: pottery, foraging, poetry, fermenting. Well, until she started going for different reasons. Best not to think about that, what's done is done. Arty folk do love Poolbeg Chimneys, don't they. Poolbeg by day, Poolbeg by night, from above, from below, from the east, from the west. They don't use them anymore of course, purely ornamental. Maybe that's the idea, keep repeating the image so that it's so embedded in the cultural psyche demolishment would be blasphemous. I wonder did people protest their initial erection, big obstructions that they are. Funny how it goes. Hard to know what will stay and what will go.

'Cause there's something in a Sunday, isn't there Johnny. That makes the body... How does it go? No matter. Something strange about this one. A 3D print of sorts. Yes, intricate layers of pattern folding behind one another like a cardboard set. Brings to mind those lively Indian diagrams you see in restaurants. Certainly draws the eye. Did that– it's moving! Now there is something new. Eyes aren't what they used to be. Is it moving? It is. It's not easy to spot, takes a moment and then something glides past, a delicate avian creature, and disappears again. Is it canvas? Framed and all. But it can't be. The material, the substance of it, looks organic. Some kind of digital gadgetry, I'm sure, and yet so tangible. Captivating. That really is something. I wonder what it feels like. Astounding the strength of the want to touch, as though still a child after all.

'They're personalised,' the artist says. A towering woman. I may not be a tall man but it's not often I feel the weight of my own head dropping back. Tall and pointy she is, with spikey grey hair – a petrified hedgehog! Ho ho. 'You upload your digital profile and, by collating your memories, experiences, desires and fears, a unique artwork is produced – just for you.'

'One of a kind.'

'It cannot be copied.'

'Sounds a bit invasive, all the same,' I look her in the eye, as best I can. Oh yes young lady, I know all about data protection, fuddy-duddy as I may appear. Donegal tweed is a choice, not a habit – it lasts. Though I'm not sure how young she is really, gifted with one of those age-defying complexions that no doubt receives regular resentful compliments.

'Your data is automatically deleted after processing,' she says seriously, maintaining eye contact, 'The artwork manifests in minutes, so you are only in the system for a very short time. I am certified. Here.' She reaches into a bag on her folding chair and hands me a business card.

Feels expensive: thick, embossed. I'll be in the system. She makes it sound like she's going to pick me up and throw me in. Not sure how I'd feel about being suddenly uprooted from the earth, legs waggling uselessly. Although I must've been picked up once upon a time, in some fairy tale a long time ago.

'If you do not like the result you do not have to buy,' she says. 'But I am sure you will like it, after all it is made for you.'

The swooning birds have appeared again, out from behind a red lace partition which ticks in languid rotation to reveal a fresh view of an elaborate baroque pattern. Tick–tick–tick. Birthdays come but once a year. Hip hip hurray! I am a jolly good fellow, am I not?

Indeed, it is customary to have a mirror over the fireplace. Expands the room. But why would I want to be looking at myself when I can view this splendid beauty? Yes, I'll take that down... Careful now, attaboy. That can go in the shed, or maybe the hallway. And up goes the, what did she call it? Something to do with light. Film, was it? Lumière... no, but similar. The Illuminator. Yes, I do like that. Whatever it means. Lighting up what? My being! And look at that, it fits perfectly. What luck. One step back and you can really see it. So bizarre. Every time I look something new is revealed although, in actuality, little seems to change. It reminds me of something. No not something, many things. But nothing definite. All are merged into one and I experience them all, as individual idiosyncratic entities. What they are I cannot recall. Recall? Strange choice of word and yet, yes, it revives long forgotten reveries. Smells even! Impossible. The distinctive smell of... What is it? Some stringent floral aroma. A sense of panic. And… delight? Stomach in flight. A dry, synthetic fizz stinging the air. What is it?

Nearly six o'clock. Better get organised. Detective Bentley won't wait. One ice for the tumbler. Measure of Tullamore Dew. Dash more for the birthday boy. Nice to receive cards today. Don't think you care until *smack* they arrive on the doormat and suddenly you've a pep in your step. Ciara will be home from Australia in a month. With her new beau. Do I hear wedding bells? She'd want to hurry up or I'll have popped my clogs before I can walk her down the aisle. Why clogs I wonder? And popped. Not really the popping sort of attire. Alright, whiskey, fags, remote. Kings? Maybe later. OK, ready for liftoff. Bentley is in a pickle once again and the stakes are high with that kid tied up the crane. What I would give for a spin in an E-Type Jag. I doubt detectives earn enough. Suspension of disbelief, Marty. Don't get bogged down in the details, after all the thug single-handedly carried a concussed preteen up a crane mast. You wonder do the actors question these things or is it understood to keep mum.

Hairspray! That's what it was. The one in the gold canister with Medusa on the front. I can smell it now. It would burn the hairs off your nostrils – heaven. God, yes. Back in the theatre days. Well, I dipped a toe in. The things you get up to and completely forget, as though it was another person altogether. I suppose it was. Kissed that woman after the show in The Mercantile, and I could go back no more. It was the adrenaline. No excuse of course, but it was. We were high as kites, flying over Dublin looking down at all the silly people and their silly little woes, all of which to us was simply fodder for our craft. No woe could touch us on stage and you'd come off it floating. Absolutely floating. The Illuminator, indeed. Stunning piece. I may have made a shrewd investment without realising it. Not so shrewd so, but no matter. It looks alive, like some organic entity sticking to the wall, free to slip off whenever it likes. I dare say it's breathing. In out, in out. Biomorphic forms dovetailing and transforming into new configurations entirely. Hypnotic. Beautiful. Truly beautiful.

That Guinness looks good and ready now, I wish he'd just bring it over already. *Good things come to those who wait.* Bloody ads would make you think they're forging the philosopher's stone. *Amateur Acting Classes. Every Wednesday, 7.30 p.m. Pepper Canister Church. Beginners Welcome!* What do they call that now... serendipity? There is a better word, more accurate. That common phenomenon explaining how you start seeing something everywhere... Whatever it is, this is that. It was probably in last week's newspaper too but only now I see it. Must be going around with eyes half-closed. Give it a circle, like a good horse to bet on. Ah here he is, Father Joe distributing the Holy Sacrament. It is ruby red too, when you hold it up to the light.

'Cheers, Joe.'

There's his pearly whites: teeth done in Turkey last February and now, no matter the mood, he is smiling. He'd be good craic at a funeral. 'Marty, a little birdy told me it's your birthday.'

Jesus, what a collision of events. How in God's name did he get a whiff of that. Who here would know? Willie maybe. He arrived on this Earth about the same time as me. A bit after, he's ever reminding me. There he is sitting with the usual suspects in the corner, Johnnie and Mick.

'That's on the house Marty,' Joe says, aggressively beaming.

'Fair play, Joe. It'll taste all the better for it.'

It does too. Why do we keep repeating each other's names? Fear we'll forget otherwise. A knock knock on the noggin, anybody home? A name is a very personal thing after all. A noise that's yours amongst all the noises. A noise to rise above all noise. *Marty Kelly.* I always thought it had a nice ring to it. Kelly is a good actor name. Doodle do do, doodle doodle do do. Acting classes. I might just.

'Here he is now, the birthday boy,' Willie singsongs. 'Thought you were getting too good for us in your old age.'

Yes, it was definitely him.

'Course not. Sure I need whipper-snappers like yourself about to make me feel young.'

He smacks his knee – literally. The Willies of the world smack their leg. Ho ho!

'Drink that down, there's another on the way,' Mick pipes up.

'Ah it's good to have friends in low places.'

I do get an odd thrill when he smacks that knee of his. The love of the crowd. Everyone enjoys a good line. *Make my day, punk.* I can see him now, summoned to life in just one line. Ol' snake eyes. But it's not just the words. Oh no. Good writers are good yes but best not inflate their egos. It's how it's delivered. Delivery is everything. A good actor is a poet, not just an entertainer. It went something like that anyway... We were always dishing out stolen pearls of wisdom at the afters, everyone offering their own carefully studied quote from the Brando Bible. Back in luvvie land. God we were a bunch of charlatans, but that was the point, wasn't it.

⫼ ⫼ ⫼

'For he's a jolly good fellow, for he's a jolly good fellow, for he's a jolly good FELL-OOOOW! WHIIII-CH nobody can deny!'

They're taking the piss now. Really laying it on. Whole pub looking. Oh don't look at them. Sure what matter. Free pints? What matter. Also it feels nice. No denying it. You love a bit of attention, Marty. No denying that. That's why you kissed her. Love the attention. Little ego needs a massage every now and again. Jesus, I'd kiss her now if she was here. But that was a long time ago. Who knows where she is, or what she looks like. Old like me, no doubt. Not how I see her. She's fixed in my mind. Forever twenty-seven, coming up for air, her little chin smudged by her own red lipstick. Pow, right in the gut. Time again. Time, time. What time is it anyway? They should be flashing the lights soon.

'Another round, good sir!' Willie barks.

'Willie, I'm done.'

'Give over, you've another pint in ye.'

'There'll be a pint coming out of me in a minute.'

'You're a gentleman.'

'What?'

'Now.' Two pints clatter down in front of me.

God, five of them in my stomach already. Looks like a sand-storm caught in a giant vial. A sandstorm running into the night. If the world was upside down, that is.

Willie sits down, releasing a squeak from his bottom as he does, 'So any wisdom to share, Marty? Looking back on it all.'

'Just the usual: follow your dreams, don't eat yellow snow.'

'Follow your dreams, still?'

'Not dead yet. I'm going to acting classes this week.'

'Jaysis, acting classes?' He says it like I'm headed for the Arctic Circle.

'Indeed. They always need a grey old man for something, I figure.'

'The next Ebenezer Scrooge.'

'I played him before!'

'You did not.'

'I did. Christmas classic. 1978. When I worked in deliveries, we had a group – a *society* we called it.'

We had three standing ovations on night two; just the right level of nerves, less than night one but enough to keep every-one bright-eyed and light-footed. Couldn't even see out from the stage, just hear the clamour of palms slapping palms, the director Ralf Wilson whistling from the back. Marianne and Ciara were down there amongst them, somewhere.

'La-di-dah. Remember any lines?'

'Bah humbug.'

'Ah don't be like that.'

Is he serious? I can't tell if he's serious. Any lines... What would be appropriate? Ah!

'I am as light as a feather, I am as happy as an angel, I am as merry as a schoolboy. I am as giddy as a drunken man.'

Willie's knee gets another beating, 'Here, here!'

'But think about that Willie, an old man happy as a schoolboy? How would you perform being that happy? A schoolboy, for Christ's sake. I can't even remember being a schoolboy.'

'Definitely not a happy one,' he snorts. Ah, too many days spent being rapped across the knees with a wooden ruler.

'A smile isn't going to cut it. And it needs to be sincere, well, *feel* sincere. This is the big moment of redemption for Scrooge, after all. You're aiming for catharsis. Do you know what catharsis is, Willie? It's when you're relieved of all your repressed anguish through dramatic art. The audience goes on Scrooge's journey with him and they too are redeemed for their faults. It's all riding on this happy ending and yet happy endings often fall flat because we don't believe in them anymore. How do you make the audience believe? I'll tell you, Willie. It's an illusion. It's all in the physicality of it. For the entire play you have to be a shrivelled up raisin of a man so that by the end just standing up straight is a dramatic contrast. A baby's first steps are a miracle to parents only because before that they're stuck crawling around on all fours. If they strolled out of the womb like a foal, it would be no big swing. It's all about context.'

Boom, boom, bam! Still got it!

⫶⫶⫶ ⫶⫶⫶⫶ ⫶⫶⫶

I had a trick for it. A tick, in fact. What was it? Now if I had a cane I could get the feel of it again. That'd shake the last forty years right off. Funny that, a cane bringing me to my youth. When canes were just props, a plaything to wield about like a dance partner. No matter, I'll use the umbrella. Yes, that's it.

And he'd kind of hang his head, but jut up his chin. Not a comfortable pose to stay in the least. Jesus, how did I manage that for two hours. Happy I took the mirror down now, wouldn't want to see the bald patch bobbing back and forth. But what was the tick? The hands, something in the hands. Yes, the money rubbing! I'd fold my right hand under my left, still holding the cane, and rub the index finger off the inner thumb. Like that. Always with the brain on the money, Mr Scrooge.

That's taken the last of it out of me. Enough of that. Maybe I'll watch a Bentley before bed. I'm not sure I even have the energy for that. It really does look like it's breathing: The Illuminator. Like those toy cats sold on Henry Street around Christmas, their little plastic chests going in and out. Company for old folks too old to take care of a real one. Could anyone really ever be too old to take care of a cat? They do most of it themselves, sure. Perhaps I should get one. I'm not too old, I don't think. Maybe no one ever thinks they're too old. Everyone else knows, awful sympathetic eyes, but you're blissfully ignorant. Well, frustratedly ignorant, caught in an endless struggle to open a jar of marmalade.

I'm looking at it again. Strangely compelling. Keeps drawing me back. A bit like a mirror actually, with me in it. Of course, I wouldn't be in it from this angle. But there is something reflective in the substance of it. Similar to that horse oil by Yeats. The brother. Something in the distance, intangible, kept drawing me back. Marianne was very patient with me that day. I think I took three bouts of the gallery, every time orbiting back to that horse as though it was the sun itself and I a confounded planet, no life left here. It was a strange jumble of feelings: awe, euphoria, a touch of sadness. And longing. Unaccountable longing. Just like this picture. Except unlike Yeats's, this one speaks back in a language of my own. As though we have conspired. As though we have always shared this pokey sitting room, it looking down on me, whispering in my ear.

⫶⫶⫶ ⫶⫶⫶⫶ ⫶⫶⫶

Blasted stone in my shoe. Out, out. Lovely to be hobbling around on one foot by Pearse Station. No holes in the sock at least. Wonder what eyes are peering out from the anonymous traffic demon. Everyone is preoccupied with themselves, Marty, you know that. Ok, the Pepper Canister. Plenty of time anyway. And it is a charming evening. Bright still. Summer nights. Yet there's a nip in the air. A northerly wind, perhaps. Enlivening. Good for the body, gets the blood working. Although those exhaust fumes can't be doing the lungs much good. It'll ease off around this corner, a lemony evening glow lighting the way, and then it'll be through Merrion which should balance the books.

Quite a few over there. The Ginger Man. Popular place. Always appears to be spilling over. I wonder do I have time… It would settle the nerves. Yes, I'd say I have time for a quick one. Make it a short. Excuse me. Think I can just about squeeze through – ah my hat! Where's it–? Ok, thank you. Could've done without the patronising smile, young lad. Yes, that's my hat. OK, here we go. Busy indeed. Probably should've gone to Kennedy's. If I can get this lady's attention now… Lowering her eyes. She sees me though. I'll give her a minute. I can always be a couple of minutes late. First time at the place, could easily have gotten lost. Here she is now.

'Tullamore Dew?'

Surveying her stock. A nod. A mute? Best not ask which one.

'With one ice cube, please.'

Please and thank you. This will do the trick. Heavenly amber elixir. Mick put me on to the stuff, fair play to him. Quite the connoisseur. Why is the mute looking at me now? Money! God, how could I forget that. It only makes the world go round. Not with it at all today. Wrong side of the bed, as they say.

Best make a move. Hold on to the hat this time. And – we're out. It was rather stuffy in there. Now for what will probably be the highlight of the evening, a stroll through the Merrion. I hope they don't make me act like a candle or something. Or a tree. Silly stuff. I want to get straight to the script. No better way to get going than to dive right in. I understand these *exercises* are meant to loosen you up but I need a character. I need to feel invested if I'm going to take all my clothes off, as it were. Would the middle path through be fastest? Doesn't bring you all the way. But it is the more scenic. Yes, why not. I can feel that warm swell now, sizzling embers tumbling over in my stomach. I hope they don't smell the drink off me. Probably should've gone for gin. No matter. Artists are temperamental, are they not. What are those young people doing? Some kind of acrobatics between the trees. Everyone's doing something. And there's yer man's so called art in the grass. Spotlights and all lighting it up. What is it anyway? Some kind of alien landing strip, like in the cornfields. Can already see it starting to fade, one blade at a time. No robin today. No little pal.

So long Merrion, it's time that we began. Now it's a straight run from here up to the church. Quite the impressive structure – three stories, positively looming. There's that word again. The terraced buildings on either side of the road look to be in jolly ceremony, redbrick soldiers about to raise their gutters in a sabre arch. Here's little old me walking between them. Hardly anyone else on the road. It appears as modest as it is grandiose somehow, on this silent street. Yes, here I am walking towards the focal point of the picture. Ionic columns gape wide, prepared to consume. Look at the size of that doorway! It would make a man feel small walking through it. Perhaps that's the point.

I wonder what time – ah, there's a sapphire clock above, keeping watch. A minute past half seven. A minute past. Such a small thing a minute. Sixty seconds. One billion nanoseconds for each second… sixty billion. Yet, undeniably, irrevocably late. And lateness becomes me… I am late. It is who I am.

I can't see anyone about. Dead really. A church seems like an odd sort of place to do it. Perhaps I have the wrong address. I'll stroll around the back and make sure there is not another entrance. That chill is getting into my chest. Rather uncomfortable.

No. No one it seems. Well, can't be expected to hang around. Maybe I'll try again next week. Yes, when this cold has shifted. Yes. No matter.

⁘ ⁙ ⁘

He shouldn't go in there. God, it's too damn dangerous. But what choice does he have? He has to know if the kid is in there. But it's too late. It's too God damn late, Bentley. That thug will be waiting. Sadistic fuck. It would be a long and painful death with him bent over you. There he is! There he is! Turn around, Bentley!

'Turn the fuck around!'

Oh no. God. Oh Jesus. That's terrible. Poor Bentley. Poor Bentley. That is so sad. Terribly sad. Terribly, terribly sad. God. Why am I crying?

⑉ ⑉ ⑉

The newspaper blows out with a satisfying crackle. Let's see. *HSE fears... Wind energy... The war...* He's at it again with the mowing. When did art become noisy. I might have a word. Give him a piece of my mind. This is a shared space after all. What do you think, Mr Robin? You probably don't mind, helps with the worm catching. But what about your singing? The ladies can't hear it over that great mechanical brute. Here, a crisp for your troubles.

I will talk to him. Yes. I'll do it now, before he gets settled. I should give that woman a talking to too. The Il-*lum*-inator, she calls it. Ah I suppose it's not her fault, I didn't have to buy it. Selling and buying, it's the way of things. In the shed now anyway, mirror back where it should be. Couldn't get used to the thing. Gave me the heebie jeebies. It was beautiful, just... It was as if it was... As though I was being... No, silly thought. It's just a painting or a print or whatever. Just an inanimate object.

'Excuse me.' Let's see what this fella has to say for himself. Can't hear me? Surprise, surprise. I'll give him a wave. Yes, hello.

'Hello,' he says. Not a kid either, in his late thirties, I'd say. Few lines on the brow, shadows under the eyes. Should know better.

226

'What is this– this thing you're doing?' Yes, give him a chance, Marty. Or enough rope to hang himself with at least. Ho, ho.

'It's an art installation, sir. It's called One Day.' Sir, he says! I know that game.

'But what's it meant to be? These wavy lines? It's causing an awful racket and I can't even tell what it's meant to be.' That's ruffled him. Put the pink in his cheeks.

'It's probably easier to make it out from over there, where those people are standing. It's a fingerprint. My daughter's fingerprint.' What's that look? Pale blue eyes checking me for something. Checking whether to say something? 'She lived for one day. That's Daisey's fingerprint.' Oh Jesus. Great. Well done Marty.

'I'm very sorry.'

'Thank you, but this is not about sympathy.'

'Oh I didn't mean–'

'Bad things, terrible things, happen all the time.'

'Indeed they do. But one day–'

'One bright lightning bolt day, forever seared into the calendar. All other days rising toward it and bowing in reverence at its leave. That's how my brother, the journalist, put it at the funeral. I think that's a nice idea, the days gathered around her. Almost like they're keeping hers company. Her one day... Greater for its brevity, perhaps. That's what I'm working through anyway. Here. Doing this. You know, humanity has only existed for about a day when compared to the universe? If you scale the chronology of the universe to a year the Big Bang happens on the 1st January and then humans only come on the scene at about half two on the 31st December. So not even a day... less.'

'Really?' Cloudy blue eyes he has, with flecks of brown.

'Yes. But if you've more than one, as we both have had, they start to blur. Don't they?'

They do.

'Tumble into each other, losing their... lustre. They become commonplace. We even wish them away. Sometimes.'

I have.

'Skipping over them to get to a favoured one and then that slips away too. Fades away as though it was never there at all.'

Blue eyes, like the Earth itself. And there I am, reflected in them.

'But that's not true,' he says, never breaking contact, billowing himself forth with every uttered word. 'It was there. That day. She was here. For one day. And for that one day, Daisey was the whole world.'

The Authors

CLAIRE BEAVER is a writer from Long Island, New York. She is the recipient of the Danielle Alyse Basford Writing Prize from Johns Hopkins University, and you can find her work in *Last Leaves Magazine*. She is an avid horror film consumer and coffee addict.

DEVON BORKOWSKI is a writer, artist, and actor from the New Jersey Pine Barrens. She graduated from Rutgers New Brunswick class of 2022, with a BFA in Visual Arts. Her poetry and short stories have appeared in numerous publications, including *The Dillydoun Reveiw*, *The Closed Eye Open*, and *Room Magazine*.

N. G. BOWIE-JOHNSON has been nominated as one of the top two storytellers by his children. When he is not trying to clinch that number one spot, he works as a business writer and instructional designer. He writes speculative fiction stories meant to feel uneasy and does not share them with his children. He has completed a Master's in Creative Writing at the University of Sydney, Australia, and, when writing bios like this, thinks maybe he should have created a website.

EMILY ISEULT DUGGAN is an emerging writer based in Donegal, originally from Dublin. In 2021, she graduated from Fine Art and Critical Cultures in NCAD. During her degree, she made sculptural installations of audio essays in Dublin City and distributed handmade zines throughout Ireland. As part of her degree show, she self-published The Eaters, an artbook of poetry, prose, audio and image, in collaboration with survivors of the Direct Provision system. This was acquired by NIVAL. Emily is currently working on her first collection of short fiction. She is a recipient of the Basic Income for the Arts.

OLIVIER FAIVRE is a French expatriate living in the Netherlands. A physicist by training, he is currently pursuing an MA in Creative Writing at the Open University.

SHANE GRIFFIN is a Dublin man who likes to write the odd story. Sometimes he writes the ordinary one too.

TOM JORDAN is a writer from Dublin. He is 25 years of age and holds a BA from Trinity College Dublin where he studied English and Drama. He writes short stories and plays. His stories have been published in *Sonder*, *The Waxed Lemon* and elsewhere.

HENRIKE LEHMEIER is an emerging writer of short fiction. Born in Goettingen, Germany, and living in Wicklow since 2001, she holds a BSc degree from University College Dublin and pays the bills baking bread every weekend in her mobile market bakery. She also identifies as a mother, hiker, runner, and amateur scientist.

ANNA MARTIN is based in Oxford, where she is studying for an MA in Creative Writing.

KURT NEWTON'S fiction has appeared in the magazines *Weird Tales*, *The Dark*, *Space & Time*, and *Daily Science Fiction*. His work has also appeared in the recent anthologies *Tales from the Ruins*, *Dangerous Waters*, *Superstitions*, and *Wicked Sick*. He lives in Connecticut with his wife and young son.

MARIA O'BRIEN is an Irish writer living in Dublin. She studied English Literature at Trinity College Dublin and has had short stories published with *Neon Hemlock* and *Kayla King Books*. Currently, she is working on a contemporary gothic novel set in the Dublin suburbs.

RAFFAELLA SERO is a writer and theatre-maker. Her fiction has appeared in *The Honest Ulsterman*, *Profiles Journal* and *Seaside Gothic*. In summer 2023 her one-woman show *The Other* will be on at the King's Head Theatre in London and at the Edinburgh Fringe. Born and raised in Southern Italy, she currently lives in Cambridge, where she is writing her PhD on Shakespeare at Newnham College.

LAYLA SAKAMOTO SHARIFI is a student, model and gremlin living in NYC. They love to read, write, make music, paint, and dance. They are obsessed with pickles, pigeons, and their dog, Sora.

POPPY SHERIDAN is a writer living in Ireland. She likes to write experimental prose and poetry that focuses on the impact trauma has on our lived experiences.

DEBORAH ZAFER lives in London with her family and rabbits. She mostly writes short fiction and is working (very slowly) on her first collection. She can be found **@deborahzafer** on Twitter or at **www.deborahzafer.com**.

www.ingramcontent.com/pod-product-compliance
Lightning Source LLC
Chambersburg PA
CBHW030933210726
48290CB00007B/2170